GIDEON'S WAY

Books by William Vivian Butler
writing as J. J. Marric
available from Stein and Day

GIDEON'S FORCE
GIDEON'S LAW

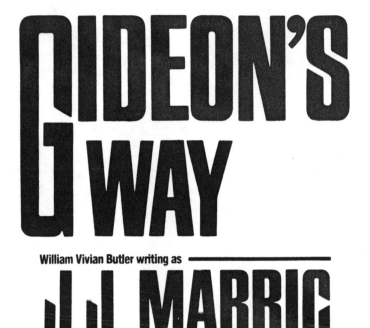

GIDEON'S WAY

William Vivian Butler writing as

J.J. MARRIC

STEIN AND DAY/*Publishers*/New York

Gideon's Way is published by arrangement with Harold Ober Associates
First published in the United States of America in 1986
Copyright © 1983 by the executors of the late John Creasey
All rights reserved, Stein and Day, Incorporated
Printed in the United States of America
STEIN AND DAY/*Publishers*
Scarborough House
Briarcliff Manor, N.Y. 10510

Library of Congress Cataloging-in-Publication Data

Butler, William Vivian, 1927-
  Gideon's way.

  I. Title.
PR6052.U875G58   1986   823'.914   85-43404
ISBN 0-8128-3075-X

To
CLAIRE and NIGEL
on their engagement
– 1 June 1982

Contents

GIDEON'S WAY

1   Back Seat

During the next twenty-four hours, Commander George Gideon of New Scotland Yard was to face, in quick succession, the trickiest turning point in his career, the gravest family crisis of his life and the most potentially explosive situation in the history of the Metropolitan Police.

But not an inkling of any of this shadowed his mind when he woke – at six o'clock, rather early for him – and lay blinking in the first sunlight of what looked like being a beautifully hot May day.

His first thought was not about crime at all, but about his brand-new grandson – a strapping blue-eyed baby that had been called George after him. Young George (all nine pounds of him) had been delivered at Fulham General Hospital just ten days before. Yesterday, Sunday, he had been driven home in the arms of his proud mother, Gideon's youngest daughter Penny, by his still prouder father, Gideon's son-in-law and Deputy Commander, Alec Hobbs. (Hobbs, for once, had been unsuccessful at hiding his feelings behind a suave, sophisticated air.) Gideon and his wife, Kate, had been privileged witnesses of the homecoming, and the climax of it – Alec holding open the front door; Penny walking over the doorstep, with a gurgling George in her arms; he and Kate following behind, with Kate almost beside herself with happiness and excitement – all this was still as clear and crisp in Gideon's mind's eye as if his brain had turned itself into an instant camera and taken a full-colour shot of it. There were other moments, too, which he liked to savour – even the one when he had ventured to tweak the baby's nose and it had responded, wrathfully, with what Alec had described as a "one hundred per cent authentic Gideon glare".

Suddenly it was as though Gideon had turned one of those celebrated glares on himself. This really wouldn't do, lying about wallowing in sentiment when there was a day to be started with a hundred jobs to be done. Since Kate was asleep and he wasn't, it looked as though Nature had decided that it was his morning to make the tea.

Pulling a dressing-gown on over his pyjamas (central heating or no, Gideon remained obstinately a pyjama man), he stumbled downstairs into the kitchen and put a kettle on. It wasn't until it was nearly boiling that he remembered that today at the Yard was going to be a rather different, and perhaps a more difficult, day than any he had known during all the years that he had been Commander of the C.I.D.

This was the Monday when Alec Hobbs ceased to be his Deputy Commander, and became instead his superior, the Assistant Commissioner (Crime).

Gideon wasn't in the least resentful of the appointment. Sir Reginald Scott-Marle, the Chief Commissioner, had repeatedly asked him to accept the post himself, but he had always declined, saying that he was too close to retirement. It was he, Gideon, who had suggested Alec for the job, and had surreptitiously been grooming him for it for months. (Not that the polished Hobbs had needed much grooming. When it came to holding his own across a conference table with the Yard's top brass, his smooth, unruffled style was almost as effective as Gideon's blunt, down-to-earth one.)

But although he was delighted with Hobbs's promotion, and had done more than anyone to engineer it, Gideon couldn't help feeling a little uneasy now that it was to become an actual *fait accompli*. The post of Assistant Commissioner (Crime) had been vacant for a long time, and before that had been held for years by an ailing incompetent. As a result, Gideon had been long accustomed to dealing direct with Sir Reginald on matters of C.I.D. policy. It would almost be true to say that he had been acting as Commander of the C.I.D. and Assistant Commissioner (Crime) rolled into one. He had been able to do this largely because Alec himself had functioned so efficiently as his deputy, taking all but the really important jobs clean off his shoulders.

Now all this was to be radically changed.

From today, Gideon was to have as Acting Deputy Commander, a new, youngish man, recently transferred from Uniform Branch, called Paul Barnaby. He had accepted Barnaby for a trial period on Alec's recommendation: when it came to choosing men for jobs, Alec was rarely wrong. But however good the new deputy might be, his style and methods were totally unknown to Gideon, and would undoubtedly take a bit of getting used to.

And – what was the point of denying it, thought Gideon – there was something else that was going to take a hell of a lot of getting used to at the Yard from now on: the fact that Alec Hobbs had the right to be consulted, reported to, and, in the final analysis, *obeyed* – on everything affecting his, Gideon's C.I.D.!

He'd get accustomed to the idea, he supposed, given time. After all, there was no one at the Yard whom he respected more than Alec – and certainly no one to whom he was closer. Sometimes it was almost uncanny how they thought and acted as one. But at other times, Alec could turn into an aloof loner, keeping his thoughts to himself. For example, he had not told Gideon any of his plans for when he became Assistant Commissioner. And Gideon could not help rather uneasily wondering why.

The whistling of the kettle broke in on Gideon's thoughts. He stared down at it, startled to realise that the kitchen was full of steam, and that there were big beads of moisture on the lid of the polished chrome teapot he was holding in his hand. The water must have been boiling for almost a minute, and yet he'd been so busy with his thoughts that he simply hadn't heard the whistling until now. If he needed any proof of how secretly worried he was about today . . .

He started to fill the pot, and suddenly there was Kate beside him, her calm grey-blue eyes watching him just a little anxiously through the steam.

"You shouldn't have come down yet, love," he protested. "I was just going to bring you up a cup."

"I had to come," Kate pointed out. "I thought at any moment the kettle would boil dry! Don't tell me you're getting absentminded in your old age."

She took command of the teapot, and in a couple of minutes they were sitting at the kitchen table, facing each other over two strong, hot cups of tea.

Kate's eyes were challenging now, as well as calm. And as usual, they seemed to miss nothing.

12

"You're worried about something, aren't you? Is it the new set-up – with Alec?"

Gideon drank half the cup before answering.

"Yes. It seems I'm more worried about it than I've cared to admit – even to myself – until now," he said. "But it's probably that I just don't like taking a back seat. And let's face it: to all intents and purposes, this is my Back Seat Day."

Kate finished her own cup, and then stood up, her tall, slim body moving with that languorous grace that never deserted her. She had always had a talent for finding the right thing to say, and that morning, it blossomed into genius.

Her eyes no longer anxious, but twinkling, she looked over his massive – and still massively powerful – frame.

"I've never known a back seat that you didn't bulge out of, love," she said. "And I don't think anyone – least of all Alec – would have it any other way."

*   *   *

It was 8.15 when Gideon left home – a red-bricked Victorian semi-detached in Harrington Road, Fulham – and about 8.45 when his large Rover nosed into the parking-space reserved for it outside Scotland Yard.

A minute or so later, Gideon was walking in through the main doors of the building. He strode purposefully, as always, but much more slowly than usual. This certainly wasn't one of those stormy Gideon arrivals which had entered into the legends of Scotland Yard – occasions when, it was said, at the mere sight of him, "better-watch-your-step" messages had been hastily passed round all departments. Now, thought Gideon grimly, the situation was completely reversed. It was he who'd have to watch his step today.

13

"Good morning, sir," said a uniformed constable behind the counter in the foyer. "I was asked to give you a message as soon as you came in. There's a meeting going on in the new Assistant Commissioner's office, and you are asked to report there straight away."

Just for a moment, it looked as though the legend was about to be reborn.

Gideon's glare caused not only the constable, but everyone else behind the counter – a sergeant and two policewomen – to turn several shades paler.

The moment of fury was quickly over, though. Gideon reminded himself that his son-in-law had a perfect right to ask him to "report" to him; and in any case, the message probably hadn't originally been put quite that way.

So he contented himself with a curt "thank you" and strode briskly towards the lifts. Twenty seconds later, entering Alec's brand-new office, he found himself confronted not only by Hobbs, but by Sir Reginald Scott-Marle himself. The Chief Commissioner – a quiet, remote man whom it had taken Gideon a long time to get to know and like – was sitting facing Alec's big new mahogany desk. Hobbs had been sitting behind it, but with a belated show of courtesy, stood up when Gideon came in.

Hobbs and Scott-Marle had two things in common: a passionate dedication to the police force, concealed by an air of casual elegance. Both turned on Gideon precisely the same bland smiles. Sir Reginald's was perhaps slightly colder, and Alec's a shade more apologetic, but that was all.

"This is really a private meeting between the new Assistant Commissioner and myself, Commander," Sir Reginald said, stressing Hobb's rank so pointedly that it was almost as if he was deliberately rubbing in the fact of Gideon's lower status. "Its purpose is to finalise certain changes that he wishes to make on taking over command. But at the last moment it occurred to Hobbs that as the changes vitally affect the C.I.D., you really ought to be called in."

In other words, thought Gideon bitterly, *until* that last moment, they had been planning to decide something "vitally affecting the C.I.D." behind his back!

"Do sit down, George." Alec, now trying hard to be conciliatory, walked round the desk and placed a chair ready for him. He was looking incredibly fresh, relaxed and immaculate for this early hour of the day - and also very young for his age. A widower in his middle forties, Alec was almost twenty years older than Penny; but this morning, it was easy to imagine that those twenty years had shrunk to ten. Was it fatherhood or promotion that had done this to him, Gideon wondered. It was probably a mixture of both. A pretty powerful mixture, he reflected. Powerful enough, perhaps, to have turned even Alec's experienced head.

Dismissing this suspicion as unworthy, he hastily accepted the proferred chair.

"To put my proposals in a nutshell," Alec began, "I'd like to make a major change in C.I.D. procedure, taking immediate effect. I am arranging for video cameras and sound recording apparatus to be installed in interrogation rooms at police stations throughout the Met area. We can't supply them to all stations at once, I know, but I understand that fifty can be equipped within a week, and between a hundred and two hundred within a month. At these stations, I'm suggesting that for a trial period, *all* interrogations should be videotaped. This will remove all risk of C.I.D. men being tempted to 'lean on' suspects they're interrogating. It'll be

15

the end of bullying inquisitors like ex-Chief Detective Superintendent Farrant. It'll also stop bogus accusations of police malpractices, like the ones that got Riddell into so much trouble during the Stannet trial last year. It was terrible to see a vice-ring leader able to laugh at the law, and drive one of our best men into a nervous breakdown.* Don't you see, George? New brooms are supposed to sweep clean – and this new broom is determined to start straight off by sweeping the C.I.D. cleaner, and clearer of suspicion, than ever before.''

Gideon remained silent for a long time. He felt like a man in a frail canoe being rushed towards Niagara.

The idea of videotaping interrogations had been under discussion for a long time at the Yard. Sir Reginald had always been in favour of it, possibly because it would greatly simplify all such things as Home Office inquiries into police conduct. Alec had long been a supporter of the idea, too, but as he very well knew, Gideon had more than a few doubts.

What would happen to the informality of police interrogations under an all-seeing electronic eye? Wouldn't suspects be inhibited from saying anything that might be even remotely incriminating? Wouldn't their police interrogators be inhibited too – mindful that the slightest slips of the tongue might get them hauled before some disciplinary tribunal?

Gideon thought of a few of his key C.I.D. men – the homely, very human Matt Honiwell; the tense, nervy but sometimes brilliant Tom Riddell; the cocky, often overconfident Lemaitre. He couldn't see any of them functioning

*Gideon's Law.

effectively in front of a video camera, yet there were no better coppers anywhere.

He was about to start arguing, when suddenly he noticed Sir Reginald and Alec exchanging resigned glances. They were sure he was going to raise objections. They were politely prepared to sit and hear him out. But they had already rejected his point of view, and nothing he said was going to affect their decision. So there really wasn't any point in wasting his breath.

"The best of luck with the experiment," he said gruffly. "For the sake of us all, I wish it every possible success. And now if you'll excuse me, I ought to be getting back to my office. There's a lot of work waiting . . . "

Trying hard to disguise his anger, he headed swiftly for the door.

*   *   *

There were two other men heading for Gideon's office at that moment. One was in a police car two miles away across London; the other was already in the lift on his way up to Gideon's floor. (He was early for his appointment, but was too tense to hang about in his own office any longer, and preferred the prospect of cooling his heels in the corridor outside Gideon's door.)

Both men were hoping desperately that, in spite of all the rumours, Gideon was still in full command.

Who else but Gideon, Chief Detective Superintendent Price was asking himself, as the lift carried him smoothly upwards, who else but Gideon would believe in his hunch that a girl (*his* girl) was in danger of being brutally murdered? All the evidence suggested that the danger was over, but yet in his bones he felt that it was still there, perhaps more acute than

17

ever. He felt something else in his bones too. No matter how difficult the task might prove, *somehow* he'd be able to find a way to convince Gideon of the continuing danger.

But if Gideon wasn't in absolute control any more, if his decisions were now to be questioned, even overruled . . .

The lift stopped, and Price got out, surprised to find that he was sweating all over. It was best not to think about things like that, he told himself, best to assume that the words on the door ahead of him still meant just what they said:

GEORGE GIDEON
COMMANDER, C.I.D.

*　　　*　　　*

Two miles away, in the trouble-spot area of Whitgate, Chief Superintendent Lemaitre was asking himself very similar questions.

The shabby Whitgate streets were looking unusually calm and bright in the 9 a.m. sunshine, but Lemaitre had a highly-coloured imagination, and kept seeing them strewn with corpses, running with blood.

And they could literally be doing that, before the end of the day . . . unless he could make someone high up at the Yard listen to him.

But the evidence was so slender that there was only one man who would - his old, old friend George, or Gee Gee, as he always called him.

The trouble was that he didn't only have to make Gee Gee listen. He had to persuade him to act - on a pretty big scale. But was he in a *position* to act on such a scale any more? If a new Top Brass had taken over . . .

Lemaitre decided to concentrate on the road ahead. That

way he could keep his eyes off those pavements . . .

A murder in one area; a massacre in another.

Totally unaware of how he was being counted on to prevent both, Gideon strode wearily into his office, determined to resign himself to his Back Seat Day.

2   Long Watch

Even in his own office there was no avoiding the sweep of the Alec Hobbs New Broom - as Gideon realised the moment he opened the door, and saw Alec's protégé, Acting Deputy Commander Paul Barnaby, standing by the desk awaiting his arrival.

"Good morning, sir. Mr. Hobbs has told me that you like to have the most urgent cases earmarked for your attention, and the relevant files placed on your desk at the start of the day."

"Mr. Hobbs has told you correctly," said Gideon, smiling as he added, "though even he never brought them in quite so early in the morning! I can see you're going to keep me up to the mark."

Paul Barnaby did not return the smile. He was definitely not the smiling type. In fact, he didn't belong to *any* type of policeman that Gideon had encountered before. Although he had only just been transferred from Uniform, he had obviously functioned there as a back-room administrator. It was very hard to imagine him in any sort of a uniform, and harder still to believe that he had ever been a constable pounding a beat. A man somewhere in his middle thirties, he had sleek, meticulously-parted black hair, a straight-from-the-cleaners flannel suit, prim, pale features and curiously round brown eyes that gave him an air of rather owlish eagerness. He might have been taken for a computer programmer, or perhaps a time and motion expert.

Just the man to work a video camera, Gideon thought sourly – and was instantly ashamed of the thought. Nothing clouded judgment like petty resentment, he told himself severely; and he had to admit he was still burning with resentment after that meeting.

He sat down heavily behind his desk, and turned his attention to the files that Barnaby had placed on its top. There were only two of them, and each had a neatly-typed memo attached, explaining why Barnaby considered that the case merited Gideon's immediate attention. The memos were models of clarity and brevity. Hobbs himself had never done better.

The first read:

THE SWANLEIGH CASE.
(Chief Det. Sup. Derek Price).
Although it is 13 weeks since Anne Swanleigh was attacked, the scene of the crime is still being kept under daily surveillance. Have suggested this is a waste of manpower. Price disagrees, and has asked to see you. Appointment: 9.30.

Gideon raised an eyebrow.

21

"*You* have suggested that Price is wasting manpower? God, man, you've only been my deputy for under an hour! Do you *have* to start by throwing your weight about?"

Barnaby blinked, and those round eyes became rather watery, suggesting that somewhere behind his bland exterior, he was nervous in the extreme. But his reply was calm and self-assured.

"Mr. Hobbs asked me to try to implement the urgent memo that Sir Reginald sent round last week, asking all departments to cut costs and use manpower more sparingly. So I took all the files on current investigations home over the weekend, and went through them with a toothcomb, looking for ways in which economies could be made. This morning, I started to ring one or two of the officers concerned. If you feel that was wrong, sir – "

Gideon struggled to be fair. Barnaby was certainly showing excess of zeal, but that was hardly to be discouraged these days.

"No, of course that wasn't wrong, and I appreciate all the slogging that it must have entailed. And God knows, with the crime rate rising every minute, we do need to be careful that we don't waste men on unproductive jobs. But please remember that in C.I.D. work, it's particularly hard to decide from looking at a file what's productive and what isn't."

"But surely, sir, in a case like the Swanleigh one, where the officer concerned never seems to have *heard* of cost-effectiveness . . . "

Gideon swallowed hard. He couldn't escape a nightmare feeling that he was being cornered; that if he wasn't careful, the very life-blood would be analysed, computerised and videotaped out of his beloved C.I.D. Back Seat Day or no, he

22

had to fight back, and the time to start was now.

He picked up the Swanleigh file, and thwacked it down again on the desk-top with all his force. Barnaby jumped as violently as if the papers it contained had been flung in his face.

"What have you learned from reading this?" Gideon demanded. "That a watch has been kept on the scene of the crime for thirteen solid weeks. A shocking waste of time and effort. Shameful waste of manpower. But things could easily have worked out differently, and through that surveillance, a very dangerous killer could have been caught, and a brave girl saved from having her head bashed in. As long as there was any chance of that, that operation was good value for money, whatever your cost analysis says."

Barnaby's eyes were beginning to water again.

"Perhaps I did give the case too cursory a glance . . . "

Gideon picked up the file again, and thrust it roughly into Barnaby's hands.

"Then I suggest you take it away," he said heavily, "and repair the omission with all possible speed."

"But won't you want the file yourself when you talk to Price?"

"No, thank you," said Gideon. "Once really learnt, the facts of the Swanleigh case aren't easily forgotten."

More than once, he'd wished to God they were. It was a sickening business which had never been far from his mind since it had begun; and some aspects of it were harrowing.

The Swanleighs had been a small family – Reggie and Dorothy, a couple in their middle fifties, with a twenty-year-old daughter, Anne. Reggie Swanleigh had been a mathematics teacher, but ten years before a brain injury received in a car crash had left him virtually paralysed from the neck down. With the insurance money, he and Dorothy had invested in a small business: a confectioner's and tobacconist's in a turning off Pimlico Road, not more than four hundred yards from Victoria Station. Dorothy had served behind the counter, while her husband had given her what she called "moral support" from his wheelchair in a little room at the back. (He was not able to operate the chair himself, but could be wheeled about in it.) Dorothy was bad at arithmetic, but only had to shout out to Reggie, and he would shout back the cost of say, a packet of cigarettes, an ounce of tobacco, three chocolate bars and a box of matches in a flash.

One cold afternoon last January, though, according to accounts given later to the police, Reggie had heard Dorothy give a different kind of shout: a sudden, sharp, desperate scream. It had struck such terror into his heart that he had been like a man possessed, and against all known laws of medical possibility, had leaped out of his wheelchair, only to fall forward unconscious on the floor of the little back room. The sound must have scared off the intruder, who had taken nothing from the till. But he had taken something of incalculable value – the life of Dorothy Swanleigh. She had been found, sprawled out over the counter, struck dead by a series of blows from a heavy blunt instrument, probably a hammer. The blows had been on the rear of her head, suggesting that she had been so unsuspecting that she had actually turned her back on the killer, perhaps to fetch something down from a shelf, perhaps to speak to her husband.

Such cases had once been extremely rare. In Gideon's early days, a killing like that would have caused a major sensation. The monster who had perpetrated it would have been the subject of a nine-day, nationwide manhunt, and no one would have rested until he was caught. But now, pointless, vicious killings of that sort were almost run of the mill. They happened twenty, thirty times a year in the Metropolitan area alone. And because they were so casual and so motiveless, the merciless yobs who committed the crimes were all too seldom found.

The Swanleigh affair, though, had had a sequel. Swanleigh's daughter Anne - who, following in her father's footsteps, had become a student at a teacher's training college - had given up a promising future to come home and take her mother's place, looking after both her father and the shop. And one afternoon - this time a grey, drizzly one in February - Reggie Swanleigh had had almost a complete repeat of his nightmare experience. He had heard his daughter give a sudden, short, desperate scream - nearly an exact replica of her mother's. This time, though, things had worked out differently. Anne had partially dodged the killer's blow, and had only been knocked unconscious. Her father had not wasted time and energy in a futile leap from the chair, but had instead used the one weapon he had - his voice - to full effect. He had, he told the police with rather pathetic satisfaction, managed such a threatening roar that the man had fled in panic. Anne had recovered consciousness before the police arrived on the scene; but her mind was a blank about the incident. She could not give even the vaguest description of her attacker. Nor did she have the remotest idea why the man should have attacked the same shop twice - always provided, of course, that it had been the same man on both occasions. It looked as though it was. The medical evidence suggested that she had been knocked out by a glancing blow, again towards the rear of the skull, from what might well have been a hammer.

One thing had stood out a mile, both to Gideon and to

Derek Price. The police must make very, very certain that they were there if the killer came again. At the same time, the best solution would be to see that if he did come, he walked into a trap. That was why the shop had been put under an immediate surveillance from a "stake-out" – a room above a long-disused dairy just across the street. That was why the surveillance had been kept up, day after day. (They'd been long days too – the shop never closed until eight.)

And that was why – if Price made out a good case for it – he would let him go on keeping it up, regardless of Scott-Marle memos and certainly regardless of the opinions of his new Deputy Commander.

But *could* Price make out a good case for it? That was the question. Much as he hated to admit it, he couldn't deny that to some extent, Barnaby was right.

Thirteen weeks *was* a long time to tie up valuable men, and the possibility of the killer attempting a third attack *was* beginning to seem remote. Unless Price could come up with some positive evidence to suggest that Anne Swanleigh was in real and continuing danger . . .

There was a tap at the door, and Price himself came in. A thick-set man of about thirty-six, he was one of the most promising of the youngish Chief Detective Superintendents on Gideon's staff. Unlike Barnaby, he had spent almost the whole of his police career in the C.I.D., rising slowly but surely from rank to rank, often as a result of Gideon's own recommendations. Few men in the department had such a record of successful arrests, yet he had a serious – and unusual – weakness as a policeman. He was bad at communicating his ideas, whether verbally or on paper. He wrote muddled, poorly-phrased reports in which, an unkind superior had once commented, the facts were "not so much marshalled as massacred''. And when talking, especially to superiors, he stammered and muttered so much that he often gave the impression that there wasn't a coherent thought in his head. (He performed slightly better in the witness-box, or he would never have secured a single conviction.) But to compensate for these drawbacks, Price had several major assets. What he lacked in clarity and incisiveness, he more than made up for in tenacity and determination. He worked on an inquiry like a dog worrying a bone, never letting go, never letting it get him down, until finally he had assembled such a cast-iron case against a criminal that nothing could confuse the issue - not even one of his own reports!

It was precisely because of this bulldog-like toughness that Gideon had given Price the Swanleigh case. It might take time, it might not be cost-effective in the eyes of people like Barnaby, but no one in the Yard was more likely to succeed in hunting that killer down.

"Good morning," said Gideon briskly, trying to ignore Price's pugnacious glare. "I understand you've been having words with my new Deputy."

"Yes. He rang me at - at half-past eight, at home, while - while I was still in the bathroom, shaving . . . Nicked my neck when - when the phone rang . . . " Price spoke in his usual half-audible manner, but Gideon was used to it, and had trained himself to catch at least two words in three.

"Very interesting," he barked. "But unless you're intending to indent for a new shirt collar, Price, I'd be grateful if you'd come to the point. Barnaby tells me that he wanted you to consider taking the watch off the Swanleigh shop. You refused and asked for an immediate interview with me. Is that right?"

Price, as usual, went off at a tangent.

"This idea of stopping the surveillance," he said, the sibilants turning his mutter into almost a splutter. "Did it – did it come from you?"

Gideon was about to reply that it didn't. Just in time, he remembered the need to be loyal to his new assistant, however much he was exasperated by him.

"Never mind where the idea came from," he barked. "The point is that it needs to be taken very seriously. Thirteen weeks you've been manning that stake-out, night and day. That's a lot of wasted man-hours, with the C.I.D. so tightly stretched." His voice softened. "I know that they haven't been entirely wasted. They've given a frightened girl and her paralysed father thirteen weeks of peace of mind. But it can't go on for ever, Derek. And unless you've a very good reason for thinking that there's still a real danger, I'm going to have to ask you to take your men off, right away."

Price's eyes widened with something like horror.

"Not right away, sir. Please give me a – a few more days. You see, I – I've finally persuaded Anne to go back to her training college. The principal's agreed to take her back even in the middle of the term. And she's making arrangements for Reggie, her father, to be looked after by his sister in Scunthorpe while she's there. So in a matter of days, the Swanleighs will be gone, and there'll be no shop to watch."

Gideon stared.

"*You've* persuaded Anne to do that? It may be a good move for her to take, but what the hell business was it of yours to – "

He broke off, seeing an embarrassed flush creep over that bulldog face. So that was it. Price had got himself emotionally involved with the girl. No wonder he'd kept on the surveillance for so long. But that didn't give him, Gideon, any logical reason for keeping it going any longer. Rather the reverse.

"Look, Derek," he said, almost as though talking to a child. "The C.I.D. is under heavy attack for wasting manpower. I ask you to justify continuing the watch on that shop. All you do is tell me, in so many words, that it might just as well continue for the time being, because the shop will be empty before long. Surely you can see that as an argument, that doesn't exactly carry a ton of weight."

Price's face went still redder, not with embarrassment now, but with a kind of desperation.

"So you *are* ord-order-ordering me to take the watch off right away."

"You haven't left me much choice," Gideon said.

"But - but - " As sometimes happened when he was really worked up, Price's voice rose, and he began to speak with perfect clarity. "I have a feeling that would be extremely dangerous, sir. Supposing that the killer is still around - and has been keeping off because he spotted the stake-out?"

Gideon raised an eyebrow.

"Aren't you crediting him with a lot of persistence, and a lot of brains, for a mindless thug?"

Price didn't give in. He never did, of course - that was his special quality.

"But supposing he isn't mindless, sir? Supposing there's a deeper motivation - a long-standing grudge against the Swanleighs?"

"In that case," said Gideon, "I'd have thought that in thirteen weeks, your inquiries should have brought the cause of that grudge to light. Didn't you tell me at one stage that you'd uncovered an ancient scandal — twenty years ago

29

Dorothy Swanleigh went off with another man, but then rebuffed him to return to her husband?''

''Yes. The man was a P.E. instructor named Anthony Marsden. But I've tracked him down, and he's happily married now, living in Yorkshire. Hardly remembers anything about the affair at all, it seems.''

''H'm. Hardly romantic, but not necessarily suspicious,'' Gideon said. ''If that's the only possible grudge you've uncovered, I'd forget this angle altogether, if I were you.''

Price was struggling for words now; with him, the struggle was spectacular.

''But I've a hunch, sir, that the murderer hasn't a normal grudge, but s-something s-s-sick, kinky, hard to des-de-des-describe – ''

''Then I'd stop trying,'' barked Gideon. ''What it all boils down to is this, isn't it? You've been keeping this watch going, week after week, simply because of a hunch, with nothing logical to back it up at all.''

Price still didn't give in – and suddenly there came a flash of shrewdness which made him, in spite of all his faults, an outstanding cop. Just when everything seemed lost from his point of view, he played a master card.

''I strongly s-suspect, sir, that *you've* followed ill-illogical hunches before now. With – with s-some success.''

Gideon stared at him long and hard. How Price had guessed it, he would never know, but it was a fact that he *did* owe a great deal to hunches. On countless occasions, they had proved crucial to his career.

He found himself grinning.

''All right, Derek, you win this one. Keep on with the surveillance for the time being, with only one officer manning it, of course. But I warn you; if any crisis comes up, calling for extra C.I.D. men anywhere in any area, the whole operation will have to go. Does that satisfy you?''

Apparently it did. The look of relief on Price's face was the first heartening thing he'd seen since arriving at the Yard that morning.

*   *   *

As Price went out, Barnaby came back into the room, and there wasn't much about his face that could be described as heartening. Except when they watered, those round eyes were as devoid of all expression as a robot's.

''I've reread the Swanleigh file as you requested, sir, but I am afraid I still can't see any case for continuing that surveillance. I did discover one rather interesting item, though. The file is cross-referenced 'VT 4072', which means that there is a cassette connected with this case in the Yard's new video library. I sent downstairs for it, and here it is.''

Gideon almost groaned aloud. Since that meeting with Hobbs and Scott-Marle, ''video'' had become almost a rude word to him.

He took the tape from Barnaby with undisguised reluctance.

''What's on this thing?'' he asked wearily. ''Price interrogating the Swanleighs? Or was there a hidden camera in here just now when I was interrogating Price? You never know at the Yard, these days.''

Barnaby, as usual, didn't smile.

''That is not an interrogation tape, sir. If so, it would have a five-oh number. Four-oh tapes like this are usually scene-of-the-crime simulations. They show police officers re-enacting a murder at the actual scene of the crime. The theory is that when the tape is run and rerun, clues might be spotted that would otherwise have been missed.''

"I know the theory,'' Gideon growled. ''What I don't know is a single case where these elaborate fun and games have brought results. Still, there's always got to be a first time, I suppose . . . Do you happen to know when this particular tape was made?''

"I looked it up, sir, and it's dated fifth January, two days after the murder of Dorothy Swanleigh. I checked with Mr. Hobbs, and he remembers that under his direction, a video camera was set up at the Swanleigh shop, and the murder was acted out in front of it, with Price as the killer and a woman police constable taking the part of Mrs. Swanleigh.''

"It sounds as though a good time was had by all,'' muttered Gideon. "But did it *do* any good? That's the question.''

Clearly, it wasn't a question Barnaby felt like tackling. He edged towards the door.

"Well, I'll leave the tape with you, sir. If you want to see it, there's a viewing room – ''

'' – attached to the video library,'' Gideon finished for him. "I don't really need a guide, you know, Barnaby – even to the *new* New Scotland Yard.''

Barnaby went out, and Gideon picked up the tape. It lay glittering darkly in his hands, in its shiny black plastic case – symbol of everything he hated about what was happening around him. For a moment, he was strongly tempted to hurl it straight into the wastebin.

Two things stopped him: a copper's lifelong respect for anything that might conceivably contain a clue . . . and a deeper, more mysterious impulse whispering that this was something he ought to see.

Shrugging, he slipped the tape into a side pocket of his jacket instead.

As Derek Price had so brilliantly divined, Gideon always paid attention to hunches.

3   Minor Case?

It was many hours, though, before Gideon was paying any more attention to that particular hunch. Within a minute, the Swanleigh tape was lying forgotten in his pocket, and he was leafing through the second of the two files that Barnaby had placed on his desk.

The memo attached to this one showed Barnaby at his most officious.

WHITGATE "POT-SHOT" INCIDENTS
(Chief Sup. Lemaitre of N.E. Divison)
This officer has urgently requested an appointment in connection with three small-scale incidents in the Whitgate area, involving random shots being fired at members of the public. He disagreed strongly with my opinion that this is a minor case, not worth your attention.

Gideon found it hard not to burst out laughing at the thought of just how strong Lemaitre's disagreement would have been. Barnaby had probably received an earful of swear-words, colourful enough to make his eyes water for the rest of the day. Lemaitre's caustic Cockney tongue spared nobody, least of all Gideon himself – and Gideon didn't expect it to, because he and Lem had been detective sergeants together near the outset of their respective careers, and had known each other far too long for any great formality to be necessary between them.

Lemaitre was a tough, shrewd detective and both qualities had been vital to him as Superintendent of one of the roughest areas of London. He had really only one weakness as a police-man: a habit of impulsively jumping to conclusions, which had led to him making misjudgments and false arrests, and so destroyed his chances of climbing any further up the promo-tion ladder. Was he jumping to conclusions now – making a major crisis out of a few minor incidents? Or was he really on to something that demanded urgent attention? The trouble with Lem was, you never knew.

It wasn't long after that when Lemaitre came in. He was looking as lean, lanky and lively as ever, although his angular features were now heavily lined, and his dark, carefully-brushed hair was becoming alarmingly thin.

"Morning, Gee Gee. Can't say I've taken to your new head cook and bottlewasher. Had to argue with him for a ruddy half hour before he even let me see you." Sinking into a chair uninvited, Lemaitre continued to vent his indignation. "Practically charged me to my face with wasting your time with a load of rubbish! I hope to God he's right, that's all I can say. Because if he isn't, and *I'm* the one that's right . . . "

Lem's voice dropped to a whisper. The life went out of his face, leaving it drawn and grey.

" . . . then there's trouble brewing, Gee Gee. The biggest

35

bloody brew-up in the history of London. And it's liable to start – tonight!''

* * *

Coming from anyone else, that statement would have been startling, even stunning. Coming from Lem, it merely left Gideon dubious and disbelieving.

He looked down again at the file on his desk. Its contents were only a couple of typed sheets, and the three incidents they described were certainly small-scale.

At about 11 a.m. the previous day, Sunday, two teenage boys climbing a fence on some waste land near Whitgate High Street had been fired at – a single shot that had passed over their heads. One boy thought it had come from a nearby roof; the other said that it had come from the back of a passing car. The waste land had been searched, but no bullet had been found.

At 2.20 p.m. someone had taken a pot-shot at a housewife standing on her front doorstep in the Colworth council estate, at the north end of Whitgate. The bullet had passed harmlessly over the woman's shoulder, and buried itself in her front door, just by the letter box. The woman had sustained a slight scratch in her right shoulder from the splintering wood just behind her, but was otherwise unhurt. She had been too taken aback to notice where the shot had come from, but the most likely firing-point was the garden of an empty house, about ten yards down on the other side of the street.

The third incident had occurred at 8.20 p.m. at a pub called The Flying Geese, at the top end of Whitgate High Street. A man had hurled open the door of the saloon bar like a character out of a Hollywood western, drawn a revolver, and fired two shots, aiming at the bottles behind the bar. He had hit none of them, but one of the bullets had ricocheted, smashed a whisky glass and nicked a barmaid's hand. She had screamed and fainted. Three customers had run after the gunman and caught him. They were still holding him when the police arrived and arrested him. He was James Mullard, twenty-six, an unemployed bricklayer who lived with his mother at 223 South Way, Colworth – not a hundred yards from where the doorstep shooting had occurred.

The report ended:

Mullard was arrested by Det. Sgt. Dewhurst at 8.30 p.m. A .38 Smith and Wesson revolver was found on him. At Whitgate Police Station, under interrogation by Det. Sgt. Dewhurst, he admitted responsibility for all three incidents, and said: "I found the gun in my coat pocket after I'd come out of a cinema. Don't know how it got there. Having got it, I just couldn't resist using it." Mullard will be charged at the North London Magistrate's Court. Is expected to be remanded for a psychiatrist's report.

Gideon closed the file and looked up, more bewildered than ever.

"A strange little case, Lem, but for the life of me I can't see why it means big trouble. Unless you've reason to think that a lot more men like James Mullard are suddenly going to find guns in their pockets when coming out of cinemas!"

He found himself grinning at the thought. But the grin faded very rapidly as Lemaitre said quietly:

"Believe it or not, Gee Gee, I *have* reason to think just that. Dick Blake, one of the best detective sergeants on my staff, was doing an undercover job last week, keeping watch on a gang of violent youths suspected of everything from rape to bank robbery. They went into the Screen Scene, a little cinema in Whitgate High Street, in the middle of the afternoon – probably just to kill a bit of time – and Blake followed them in. Now when he's on that sort of work, Blake gets himself up to look like the most vicious type of yob. And he really does a complete Laurence Olivier acting job: wild hair, twisted lips, blank, staring eyes – the lot. Well, there he was, sitting in the cinema about ten seats behind his quarries, when a man comes sidling up and takes the seat next to him. A bit of a liberty, Blake thought, seeing that he was all by himself in the row . . . and he was prepared for some homosexual funny business." Lem suddenly stood up, his face graver than ever. "There was some funny business all right, but it wasn't sexual. The man started to press something into his hand. Blake couldn't see what it was in the dark, but it felt cold, hard and metallic – like a gun."

"Didn't he try to arrest the man?"

"No. When Blake refused to accept the object, whatever it was, he was gone in a flash – and he couldn't very well give chase, could he, because it would mean blowing his cover.

"There's one more thing I ought to mention, Gee Gee – and I think it'll make your hair curl, what's left of it. The film being shown was an X-rated picture called *They Killed For Thrills*, about a gang who take pot-shots at passers-by from the back windows of cars. Blake reckons – and I agree with him – that someone is deliberately studying the audience at each showing of that film. And every time he sees a mentally subnormal type, sitting alone and staring up at the screen as if mesmerised, this man sidles up and slips him a loaded gun."

Gideon's hair might not have been rising – but little shivers were shooting up his spine and round his scalp.

"But what in God's name for? And in any case – where would he get the guns and the ammunition?"

Lem's face was suddenly as grim as he had ever seen it.

"The second question is easier than the first. There are a lot of guns turning up all over Whitgate these days – and bullets too. Special Branch thinks that some organisation is bringing them in by the crateful."

"What organisation?"

"I can give you two guesses, Gee Gee – and either of them could be right! Remember, Whitgate has the dubious honour of being the home of *both* of the most extreme political factions in Britain. On your left, you've got a load of raving reds calling themselves the Workers Unity Wing. Leader: one Jeremy Caxton, a lovable lad who never mentions the police without calling us 'the SS of the Fascist Establishment'. On your right, you've got the Back to Great Britain Movement, or BGBM for short. Leader: Sir Gilbert Fordyce, who wants to bring back *public* hanging – with Jeremy Caxton as the first man on the scaffold, as far as I can make out. It may sound funny, but it's no bloody joke being in the centre of this mess, I can tell you. We don't get riots in Whitgate. We get pitched battles with bottles thrown, shop windows smashed and an average of half a dozen serious injuries every night. And tonight it could be a hell of a lot worse. A local by-election's been announced, and Caxton and Fordyce are both speaking at meetings in the Civic Centre – in halls that are practically next door to each other! It only wants one of these pot-shot maniacs to show up – and aim at, say, Caxton or Fordyce or one of their top supporters – and there'll be a situation that doesn't bear thinking about."

"But we've got to bear thinking about it, Lem," said Gideon softly. "And if it's any consolation, my thoughts are now exactly the same as yours. This case could turn into something very far from minor."

Just for a moment, a smile of satisfaction flickered over Lem's thin, sharp face.

"Not jumping to conclusions this time, was I, Gee Gee?" he said triumphantly.

But there was fear, not triumph, in his eyes as he added, hoarsely:

"Someone *is* trying to start a bleeding civil war!"

4   Veto

Poor old unchanging Lem, thought Gideon. He'd boasted
about not jumping to conclusions, and in almost the same
breath, had jumped to the most alarming conclusion of his
life!

"Take it easy," Gideon said, as sternly as if he were
speaking to a young trainee constable. "The way I see it, this
thing is a lot more mysterious than that."

Standing, he began pacing up and down his office, something he only did when he was alone, or with a very old
friend. (Despite their difference in rank, he had put Lem into
that category years before.)

"Let's suppose you're right, and someone *is* out to stir
things up - to make the whole of Whitgate explode into open
street warfare. And let's suppose that he knows where he can
get his hands on a supply of guns and ammunition. Well,
surely the logical thing for him to do would be to send
gunmen to political meetings, or get them involved in street
fighting. Sidling up to weirdos in cinemas and slipping guns

into their hands or pockets at random is the craziest way of going about it that one can imagine. Men like that are liable to shoot at anything or anybody, from a lamp post to a lollipop lady – but there's no guarantee they'll go anywhere near a political gathering, and if they don't, a hundred pot-shots won't start your civil war!''

Lem stood up and looked for a moment as if he would join in the pacing. But he remained still, only his sharp eyes moving as they followed Gideon's progress around the room.

''Oh yes they will, Gee Gee,'' he said tensely. ''You don't know what Whitgate's like these days. With streets of closed warehouses and factories, unemployed kids of all colours on the prowl in gangs, and political loonies forming cells and collecting guns, the place is a powder keg just waiting for the first lighted match to be thrown in. It was bloody lucky that Mullard's shots missed everyone he aimed at. If he'd hit that housewife, or those schoolboys, or the barmaid at The Flying Geese, there's no telling what he might have started.'' Suddenly, he stabbed a finger in Gideon's direction. ''And if you want to know *why* a troublemaker should use such round-about methods, I've got an answer to that too. Supposing he is himself a member of the Back to Great Britain Movement, or the Workers Unity Wing. If he got his fellow fanatics to start the shooting, that could very easily be traced back to him. But by using an army of near-nutters, who don't even know how they came by their guns, he's as safe as ruddy houses . . . even if the whole of Whitgate disappears in gun-smoke!''

Gideon stopped pacing abruptly, halted in his tracks by that stabbing finger – and the shrewdness and force of Lem's arguments. He still wasn't by any means sure that Lemaitre's conclusions were right. But he was beginning to feel that they *could* be. And that was enough to start alarm bells ringing down all the corridors of his mind.

Special Branch would have to be alerted. House-to-house searches for guns ought to be started immediately in all the known trouble-spot regions. Area-car patrols should be trebled throughout Whitgate. Uniform would have to be prepared to turn out in force to the two political meetings at the Whitgate Civic Centre tonight. And it might be necessary to take the unusual step of having a good proportion of those uniformed men armed.

He disclosed these plans to Lem, adding: "And if I were you, I'd start getting pretty busy round that cinema – what's it called, the Screen Scene. It's possible that our quarry hasn't realised that he's been rumbled, in which case he may be back handing out more guns. You're planning to station men in the audience at all future performances of this sick film, I imagine. But I think you also ought to question everyone attached to the place, from the manager to the ice-cream girls. They may well know a lot more local weirdos, by sight or by name, who are regular cinemagoers. Any one of them could by now be carrying a gun."

Lemaitre stood up, obviously anxious to get back to Whitgate. His haggard expression had gone, replaced by an eager, excited look that Gideon had not seen on his face for years.

"Count on me," Lem said breezily, adding with an unusual display of emotion for him, "It's only right. Whenever I'm in a fix, I always know I can count on you."

As soon as the lanky Cockney had gone, Gideon reached for the phone. An operation involving not only the C.I.D. but Special Branch and Uniform would require top-level authorisation. Without thinking, he began to dial Scott-Marle's extension.

Suddenly he stopped, remembering the new protocol. It was Alec, not Scott-Marle, with whom he had to liaise now.

Good, he thought. It was true that Alec was in a strange mood this morning, seeing himself as this bristling new broom sweeping away all the cobwebs in the C.I.D. But they had worked together so long and knew each other so well that in an emergency like this, they were bound to see eye to eye, both about what was at risk and what needed to be done.

Alec did not answer the phone himself. He was now one of the few men in the building entitled to a secretary, and had obviously lost no time in engaging one. A brusque, unfamiliar female voice informed Gideon that the Assistant Commissioner was very busy, but would try to "fit him in" for a few minutes, if he would come to his office straight away.

"Warn him that I'll be a tight fit," said Gideon grimly.

In fact, it took him nearly twenty minutes to repeat to Alec all that Lem had told him, and to outline his proposals.

And it took Alec – smooth, calm and courteous as ever, but otherwise an alien being utterly remote from his former Deputy Commander – just two minutes to turn down each and every proposal.

*　　　*　　　*

"I'm sorry to do this to you, George, more sorry than I can say. But to be brutally frank, I think you're trying to turn a minor case into a major alert, without having any real justification for doing so. A mentally subnormal pot-shooter says that he *thinks* he found a gun in his pocket after leaving a cinema. A detective sergeant claims, after a visit to the same cinema, that someone pressed something cold and metallic into his hand for just a moment in the dark. On those two incredibly flimsy bits of evidence, you're practically asking me to call out the guard, read the Riot Act and declare martial law!''

Gideon stood up angrily from his chair and towered over the seated Hobbs.

''I hardly think what I've suggested amounts to that.''

Alec did not stand. On the contrary, he leant back in his chair – a brand-new revolving one, of the plushest leather – and folded his arms, a relaxed gesture, confident rather than defiant.

''Doesn't it, George? Trebling area-car patrols, and packing political meetings with a heavily-armed contingent of uniformed men comes pretty close to it, in my view. And conducting house to house searches for arms in all the trouble-spot areas is hardly likely to cool tempers and keep things calm. We'd be wasting a lot of men, a lot of time and a lot of money on one of Lem's most extravagant whims, and coming close to causing the very explosion he fears!''

Then Alec *did* stand. Not abruptly, but very casually and elegantly, he rose to his full height. He did not have Gideon's massive presence, but his calmness and coolness gave him an impressiveness of his own.

''Time, men and money are not going to be squandered on whims by anyone in the C.I.D. from now on. We're facing such a continual minute by minute increase in crime, that we have to husband our resources as never before.''

''By installing video cameras at police stations – at around five thousand pounds a time?'' barked Gideon.

It was an angry question, with all his pent-up fury behind it – but Hobbs didn't turn an elegant hair.

''That's part of it, George. If Scott-Marle and I can see for ourselves what men have said under interrogation, we can much more easily keep tabs on what's happening in any

45

particular case – and make sure the officer concerned is conducting it efficiently. Besides that, I am going to start daily scrutinies of cost-effectiveness across the whole department. Chief Detective Superintendents will be asked to justify their activities, in terms of time and manpower spent, in far greater detail than before. They'll have computers to help them, of course. In fact – '' Alec's calmness suddenly gave way to an eagerness approaching excitement '' – they'll have a vast range of new equipment to help them, in every area of their work.''

Like videotaped scene of the crime simulations, thought Gideon sourly. He had a nightmare feeling that the real Alec Hobbs had been spirited away, and that he was actually talking to Paul Barnaby in disguise.

Some hint of his own confusion and consternation must have appeared in his eyes, because Alec's tone suddenly changed. His voice softened, and became almost pleading.

''I knew you wouldn't take kindly to any of this, George. That's why I didn't let you in on my plans in advance. But don't you see? That's the only direction the C.I.D. can go in, if it's to become an effective crime-fighting unit in this day and age. We just can't afford to do things any longer in – in – ''

He broke off, too embarrassed to continue.

It was left to Gideon to finish the sentence for him.

''In the Gideon way?'' he asked bitterly.

And had stormed out of the room before the new Assistant Commissioner could reply.

*　　*　　*

As soon as Gideon was back in his own office the phone rang and Lemaitre was on the line.

''Thought I should tell you, Gee Gee, that I'm setting up a

temporary headquarters at Whitgate police station. It's just across the road from the Civic Centre, so I'll be well placed if any trouble starts tonight.''

"Pray that it doesn't start," said Gideon softly. "Because if it does, Lem, I'm afraid we're all going to be caught with our trousers down.'' And he added savagely, "By order.''

It never took Lem long to read between the lines.

"You mean – you got no change out of the new top brass?"

Gideon hesitated. He did not want it to get about that he was at odds with his own son-in-law. But he needed to be frank with somebody; and after all, Lemaitre was his oldest associate.

"Not a halfpenny," he confessed. "All my proposals were vetoed, on the grounds of insufficient evidence to warrant a major operation. It might change things if more reports of random pot-shots come in during the course of the day, but I wouldn't count on it. There haven't been any incidents so far, I take it?''

"None," said Lemaitre. "And there wasn't even the slightest skirmish between Lefties and Righties on the streets last night. Everything's gone quiet . . . ominously quiet, it seems to me."

"It doesn't have to be ominous," Gideon reminded him. "It may simply be that Hobbs is right and we're wrong about the whole situation. Mullard could have stumbled on that gun by accident; Blake might have been imagining things in that cinema; you might have been exaggerating about the tension in the air . . . ''

"And at those political meetings tonight, Sir Gilbert Fordyce and Jeremy Caxton might just join hands, and start dancing round the Maypole!" Lem snorted. "Don't be fooled, Gee Gee – there's trouble on the way all right, and it looks as though we're helpless to stop it.''

"H'm," said Gideon. "Did you get anywhere with questioning the cinema staff?"

"No. The place is shut till twelve. I'll be round there as soon as it opens, though – and I've got men on standby to watch all performances of *They Killed For Thrills* throughout the day." A thought suddenly struck him. "By the way, Mullard's been before the beak and, as I expected, he was remanded for a psychiatrist's report. There's a few people at the Yard needing one of those this morning, if you ask me!"

Gideon decided it would be disloyal to be heard agreeing with that.

"I'm *not* asking you," he grunted, and slammed down the phone. He stood up and walked over to the window.

The morning was getting hot. Already it was more like June than May. Everything – from the clock face of Big Ben high above to the streams of red double-decker buses moving down Victoria Street far below – seemed to be swimming in a shimmering haze. The scene had an unreal, mirage-like effect which was heightened by the fact that the new Scotland Yard building had very efficient sound insulation, and no traffic noises penetrated into the room.

Gideon had a sudden nostalgia for the old Scotland Yard, where on hot days like this all the sounds of London – newsboys shouting, river tugs hooting, buses rumbling, Big Ben booming – would pour in through the open windows. The super-efficient silence of the new building – where, because of air conditioning, all windows were permanently closed – was fine for working in of course, but there were times when it became oppressive, and this was one of them. He couldn't escape the feeling that the whole of London had become like Lemaitre's Whitgate - ominously quiet.

He turned away from the window back to his desk and sat down, telling himself not to be so ridiculous. This was just a reaction from all the shocks of this shattering morning. But despite all his efforts, the feeling grew that there were many kinds of menace abroad in the bright May sunshine . . . and that some of them were creeping up, closing in.

He slipped a hand in his jacket pocket, in search of the old pipe that he always kept there. He never smoked it now, but when troubled by anything, he liked to turn it over in his hands, and sometimes to bring it out and clench it between his teeth. His fingers brushed against the video tape of the Swanleigh murder, and made him think of Derek Price. Was that odd young copper's strange hunch right? Was Anne Swanleigh's attacker, and her mother's murderer, waiting for a chance to return? If so then he, Gideon, had only just stopped the Yard's new cost-effectiveness policy from costing a life!

And it could still cost lives - perhaps dozens of them - if Lemaitre was right, and someone in Whitgate was determined to spark off street warfare on a scale never known in Britain before.

Yes, there were many kinds of menace around all right. But just because they weren't the kinds that registered on computers or showed up on video tapes . . .

The telephone rang at that moment, making Gideon jump. His jump startled him more than the bell. He'd had no idea his nerves were in such a state.

But it was only Kate, calling to tell him that she was spending the day at the Hobbs's house in Hurlingham. Penny had long ago blossomed out as a concert pianist, of such quality that she often performed with the B.B.C. Symphony

Orchestra. Today, it seemed, she was wanted at a recording studio, to play again some passages which had been faultily taped the last time she was there. Not the sort of chore that was very welcome on the day after one came home from hospital with a newborn baby, but Penny was nothing if not a professional, and had agreed to go, if her mother would baby-sit. Kate, of course, had been more than willing to oblige – and Gideon found himself listening to a long, glowing account of how beautiful baby George was, and how perfectly he was behaving.

At any moment he thought that the baby would be brought to the phone to gurgle a greeting in person, but apparently he was in his pram out on the lawn in the Hobbs's garden.

"It's too nice a day for him to stay inside, don't you agree?" Kate said. "I've been lying on the lawn beside the pram . . . It's so hot out there that I'm almost tempted to borrow one of Penny's swimsuits and start sunbathing. Or do you think that sort of thing's ridiculous at my age?"

"Ridiculous?" Gideon grinned. "All that's worrying me, love, is that with your figure, you might be giving the neighbours too much of a treat."

He replaced the receiver with Kate's laugh still ringing in his ears – and with his mood completely changed.

Joy at the thought of his brand-new grandson flooded through him, softening his bitter feelings about Alec and driving all the forebodings of menace clean out of his brain.

Yet ironically, it was upon that brand-new grandson that, at that very moment, the darkest kind of menace was closing in.

5 Kinds of Menace

Menace was, in fact, closing in on many people around London on that bright May morning, though almost everywhere it was at first underestimated, undetected or ignored.

The last thing on Kate Gideon's mind as she breezed upstairs to her daughter's bedroom in search of a swimming costume, a pair of sunglasses and perhaps some suntan lotion, was that it might be dangerous to take her eyes for one second off the baby George. The pram was on a flat, firm stretch of lawn; she had checked the brakes; and of course he was too young to be able to move about and fall out by accident. She was well within earshot if he should happen to start crying, and in any case would be back in under two minutes.

In the event, she was back in under one. The moment she stepped into the bedroom, which was on the side of the house facing the road, she saw a large black Ford Capri pulled up by the side gate leading into the Hobbs's garden. The left-hand back door of the car was open, and the driver was keeping the engine running.

She had a faint, shadowy impression that there was somebody else on the scene, someone in the back of the car, directing operations, but keeping well away from any of the windows.

From that one quick glimpse – a half or even a quarter-glimpse, lasting only a microsecond – she had the even more shadowy impression that there was something familiar about him. But she thrust the thought instantaneously out of her mind as fanciful, absurd.

What wasn't fanciful – what was as stark and clear and unmissable as the black Capri itself – was the fact that something criminal was going on.

The car looked almost like a getaway vehicle waiting for a gang to return from holding up a bank.

But there wasn't a bank within miles. In any case, if they'd come to steal money, they'd have stopped outside the house, not the side gate into the garden.

What was there to steal there except – except –

Surely it couldn't be the *baby* –

In something like blind panic, Kate rushed out of the bedroom, back down the stairs, and out onto the lawn.

*   *   *

Five miles to the north, on the edge of Pimlico, menace was equally far from the mind of Detective Sergeant Peter Potter, the man on surveillance duty across the road from the Swan-leigh shop.

He had taken up his position in the stake-out – a small, dusty room above a long-closed dairy – three hours before, at nine o'clock. He knew that he was supposed to record every customer who called at the shop, writing down a brief description, time of arrival and time of departure. But he had performed this wearisome chore so often in the past three months that now he was quite shamelessly coming the old soldier. Caller after caller went unrecorded, while he read a newspaper or just stared at the cracked, stained ceiling. Sometimes an hour went by without him glancing across at the shop at all.

He knew, of course, that if his superior, Chief Detective Superintendent Derek Price, caught him cheating he would have his guts for garters. But Potter, a shrewd young man when he wasn't bored or frustrated, believed that Price's guts were in far greater danger of being gartered than his own. If word got out that Price was wasting his men's time on this useless surveillance for week after week, just because he fancied the Swanleigh girl . . .

For the hundredth time that morning, Potter opened the *Sun.*

He had just turned to page three and was about to run his eyes over today's topless beauty for at least the thirtieth time, when Anne Swanleigh's scream rang out across the street.

*   *   *

About two miles further north across London, walking through one of the shabbiest and most decayed streets in the closed-factory area of Whitgate, Constable Charles Morton should by rights have been acutely aware of menace, or at any rate of the possibility of attack.

In fact his fat red face was wreathed in smiles at the prospect of the ham pie salad that awaited his arrival home for lunch.

Charlie Morton was now in his late fifties, and had been very content to remain a constable all his life. He was one of those *comfortable* policemen, a type which is rare now, but was extremely common once – so common that it was parodied in endless books, films and plays, and usually made to say "Nah then, what's all this 'ere?" on the slightest provocation. He looked as if he would be at home in some rural village, and was hopelessly out of place in this filthy, rubble-strewn street. But appearances were deceptive. Charlie had been born and brought up in Whitgate. He loved the place, and had a gift for handling the people here.

His natural warmth and joviality made him surprisingly popular with gangs of youths, black or white, Left or Right. If they followed him about, making faces as they sometimes did, he was likely to react not with a glare or a threat, but by shaking with laughter . . . laughter so infectious that they would end by joining in.

Not that even Charlie could find too much to laugh at in Whitgate these days. His homeward route took him past an old brick bus shelter, and the sight of it made him groan aloud. Once upon a time, this had been a very busy shelter, and he even had sentimental memories of it: he had seen his future wife, Mavis, off on a bus here many a night in their courting days, and he would never forget those kisses in the dark before that last bus came . . .

Now, though, the shelter was out of use, because the buses had been rerouted after the closure of all the factories in the road. *Some* folk still had a use for it, it seemed. The dirty brick walls were a mass of political posters and scrawled graffiti. The features of Sir Gilbert Fordyce on the Back to Great Britain posters, and of Jeremy Caxton on the Workers Unity Wing ones, were equally slashed, daubed and decorated; but even blacked-out teeth and comic specs and moustaches could not hide the blazing fanaticism in the faces of both politicians.

Fordyce's face was of the stern, military type; Caxton's had a
lean, hungry intensity. But both seemed to be staring imper-
iously out of their posters, threatening passers-by to come to
their respective meetings tonight at the Civic Centre – or else.

Scrawled all round the posters, and covering almost every
inch of the brick wall at the back of the shelter, were graffiti
messages of every kind, from *Forward With Fordyce* to *Spurs
Rool - Okay?* At the very top of the wall, just below its
junction with the roof, was a stark three-word command
sprayed in vivid scarlet paint. It had obviously been put there
by one of the most vicious of the yobbo gangs, and simply said,

KICK TO KILL

By this time, Charlie's slow, measured pacing had brought
him directly in front of the shelter. He started. A boy – he
looked to be about sixteen or seventeen – was actually trying
to add something to the topmost message at that very
moment. He was standing on the shelter's one remaining
wooden seat, struggling to reach up high enough. He was
only about five foot three inches tall, so the struggle wasn't
easy. It was taking up all his attention, and he was quite
unaware of the constable's presence behind him.

Charlie Morton folded his arms and waited patiently for the
youth to notice him. Suddenly the situation struck him as
funny, and he started to shake with laughter. The youth
didn't seem to hear a thing. He was too busy sending a stream
of scarlet paint up to the top of the wall. He succeeded in
blotting out the word KICK and then started to add a word
of his own below it. Charlie watched as he sprayed the letters
SHOO.

"SHOO, eh?" he said, jovially. "That's a good idea
you've got there, Laddie. You shoo off and scarper home

as quick as a flash, and leave other people's walls alone in future. Otherwise, I'm afraid I'll have to shoo you along to the police - "

He broke off, his chortle turning into a startled gasp as the boy swung round and hurled the can of spray paint straight at his face.

Charlie was agile for his size. He ducked, and caught the can as smartly as though it were a cricket ball. But the results weren't so neat. Scarlet paint spread all over the front of his uniform. Contact with the blue turned the colour crimson, and made it look almost as though he was bleeding from a chest wound.

He kept his temper, as he nearly always did.

"That was a bit naughty, lad," he said. "But I'll make allowances, because I suppose I did creep up on you, so to speak. As long as you get down from that seat and are out of my sight in five seconds - "

Again he broke off with a gasp.

For the first time, he'd had a proper look at the boy's face. It was white and mask-like, totally without expression except for the eyes, which were blazing with a hatred more intense than Fordyce's and Caxton's put together.

Abnormal, thought Charlie. Dangerously abnormal . . .

For once he felt uncomfortable, a feeling that turned sharply to outright fear as the boy produced a revolver, and sneered:

"You should have let me finish my bit of writing, copper. Then you'd have known my motto. SHOOT - TO - KILL."

6 Kinds of Fear

Charlie suddenly remembered a story that was going round the station that day, about someone handing guns to crazy yobbos in cinemas. He had laughed at the story when he'd heard it. It didn't seem quite so funny now.

Nothing, in fact, seemed funny now at all. Nevertheless, Charlie began chortling, partly because laughter had so often made friends of youthful enemies, but mostly because it was the only way he could think of to hide the fact that his portly frame was shaking with fright.

"You don't want to lark about with things like that, son," he said, and somehow succeeded in sounding his usual, comfortable self.

"Better give it to me, quick," he added, stretching out a right hand which was only just a shade unsteady. "And if I find it's loaded, I'm afraid I'll have to take you in."

The mask-like mouth actually creased into a smile.

"You'll find it's loaded all right, copper," the boy said.

Just as he'd seen the pot-shooters do in the movie, he

raised the safety catch of the revolver, and fired at point-blank range.

Almost before Charlie's body hit the ground, he had sprung down from the seat, pocketed the revolver and scooped up the spray-gun. Then he jumped up on the seat again, and turned back to the wall.

He couldn't leave, he told himself, until he'd put that T in SHOOT TO KILL.

*   *   *

At that precise moment, Detective Sergeant Potter was halfway across the Pimlico backstreet which ran between the police stake-out and the Swanleigh shop. Anne Swanleigh's scream had not been repeated, but it was still ringing in his ears, and blasting through his brain with the force of an alarm klaxon at a nuclear plant.

If, after all these weeks, the killer was paying a third visit to the shop, and had walked into the place unnoticed while he, Potter, had been lolling about and reading page three of the *Sun,* the consequences didn't bear thinking about. For him. For the girl. For anyone . . .

Panic. He mustn't panic . . . even though time was standing so still that he might have been in a nightmare. Every step seemed to take an hour – and even when he'd taken six, seven, perhaps eight paces, the shop still looked strangely far away: a ghost shop, silent as death in the brilliant sunlight, its door swinging slightly but soundlessly to and fro, giving no hint of what, if anything, was happening inside.

Was the girl dead? Would he find her, sprawled out over the counter with her head bashed in, the way her mother had been found, and she herself had almost been found, the last time?

Would the killer still be there, standing over her, claw-hammer at the ready to strike again – this time at him? Or would the man have gone out the back way, perhaps attacking Anne's invalid father en route?

Guilt and fear combining to bring him close to terror, Potter hurled himself across the rest of the street, and flung the shop door open so violently that he nearly cracked the glass.

Once inside the shop, he stood, breathless, for several seconds, staring blankly at Anne Swanleigh, who was leaning against the wall behind the counter, as white as though she'd just seen a ghost, but otherwise quite unhurt.

There was no one else in the shop, but sounds of alarm were coming from the back. Reggie Swanleigh was asking very agitatedly if his daughter was all right.

"Are you – all – all right?" Potter stuttered, his nerves making him sound almost like his despised superior, Price.

"Yes, yes, really. I'm sorry I screamed like that. It was nothing, nothing at all."

Obviously making a great effort to pull herself together, Anne moved away from the wall and stood, arms folded, staring at him across the counter. She was a slim, slightly-built brunette with a reserved, rather prim air, probably due to shyness or perhaps, simply, to fear. After all, Potter remembered, she was standing on the very spot where her mother had been murdered, and where she herself had been knocked unconscious, probably by her mother's killer. For the first time, Potter began to understand why Price had not been in a hurry to close down the stake-out and he even felt a certain sympathy with that decision.

There was a moment's silence. Old man Swanleigh in the back room had stopped calling out; obviously, the sound of

59

his daughter's voice had told him what he wanted to know.

Potter tried to smile reassuringly. But he was still too shaken up for the attempt to be successful. All he managed was an awkward half-smile that looked as if he were suspicious. And his voice came out as a bark when he said, "All that was about – nothing? That's going to look pretty stupid in my report!"

Anne paused for another long moment. Then hesitantly, almost apologetically, she pointed down to something on the floor at her feet, behind the counter. Potter opened the flap, and walked behind the counter himself. Only then could he see what she was pointing at. It was nothing very alarming – just a child's rubber ball, rather a big one, about six inches in diameter.

There was a rack of rubber toys, from balls to ducks, from grinning fish to scowling Miss Piggys, in a six-foot-high rack just by the door at the back of the counter. Confectioner-tobacconists often carried lines like that these days, probably to compensate for the diminishing returns from cigarettes.

Potter picked up the ball and twirled it between his fingers. It was bright red with yellow stripes; the colours, he remembered for no reason, in which he played football on the rare occasions when he got a Saturday afternoon off . . .

"*This* is what frightened you?" he said, unable to hide his amazement.

"Yes. It – it suddenly came bouncing off that rack. I was showing a ball to a child who was in here just now. I suppose I hadn't put it back properly afterwards. I don't know why it startled me so much. But – something about it seemed to remind me – of – "

"Of what?" Potter asked quietly.

The shrewd, ambitious side of his brain was working overtime. He knew that a key stumbling block in this inquiry was the concussion which had blacked out all Anne's memories of her attacker. If he, Potter, could be the one who started those memories returning . . .

Gently, as if just for fun, he began to throw the ball up in the air and catch it. Anne followed it with her eyes as if it mesmerised her - but then, abruptly, the spell broke.

"Please don't do that," she said sharply, so sharply that he started - and dropped the ball.

That was when the extraordinary thing happened.

The ball fell out of his hands and bounced first on to the counter and then out into the shop, where it bounced around the floor.

As it did so, Anne put her hands to her face - and then screamed again, almost as loudly as before.

The next moment there was uproar, with Anne sobbing and Reggie Swanleigh shouting at the top of his voice from the next room:

"What's going on? What are they doing to you? Come in here and let me see you . . . "

Without another glance in Potter's direction, Anne went through the door at the back of the counter, and all he could hear after that were her sobs and the sounds of Reggie Swanleigh trying to comfort her.

His efforts seemed to be taking the form of stern fatherly advice.

"Try to act like my daughter. However tough things are, *I* don't go all to pieces - even in my condition . . . "

My God, thought Potter. The girl was on the edge of a breakdown, and he'd nearly pushed her over it. The best thing he could do was get out of here - fast.

Ten seconds later, he was back in the stake-out across the

road, feeling more panicky – and more guilty – than when he had rushed out from it, two minutes before.

To relieve his sense of guilt, he screwed up the newspaper and threw it across the room. From then onwards, his eyes never left the front of the Swanleigh shop.

They did not even leave it when he stepped across to the police transmitter (a type specially made for stake-out use) which stood on a trestle table at the back of the room.

At the touch of a button, he was in direct contact with Derek Price at Pimlico police station. Apart from routine reports when men came on or went off duty, it was the first time the stake-out had made contact with the station since the surveillance had begun, the first positive development on the case in thirteen blank and weary weeks.

A very tense and excited Price stuttered, "What – what is it, Potter? Anne . . . is Anne all right?"

For the second time that morning, Potter found his own voice as hesitant and stumbling as his superior's.

It was hard to explain that all he was ringing about was a bouncing rubber ball.

*   *   *

At about the time when Anne Swanleigh had been staring, mesmerised, at the ball in Potter's hand, Kate Gideon was staring, equally mesmerised, at the pram at the end of the Hobbs's lawn.

She didn't have to go a step nearer to see that it was empty. It was, in fact, lying on its side, with blankets and pillow spilling out across the grass, and two of its four wheels still spinning in the air, the whirling spokes a dazzling blur in the hot sunlight.

Suddenly the whole scene became a blur to Kate as her eyes

filled with tears of fear, panic, desperation. She tried to rush across the lawn, but stumbled blindly into a canvas garden chair and fell headlong across it. As she struggled to pick herself up, there was a terrible moment when it seemed she couldn't think or feel any more than she could see. And it was during that moment that she heard a car start up outside the garden gate, and go roaring off at what sounded like all of sixty miles an hour.

Roaring off – with the baby George . . .

That thought changed Kate, in a flash, from a distraught grandmother into the wife of a C.I.D. Commander. By the time she had got to her feet her eyes were drying and her brain was clear. What was the point of blundering blindly around the garden? She needed to get indoors – fast – to telephone.

She ran back into the house, her thinking now coherent, if far from calm. She could give a clear description of the black Capri, which was something, at any rate. If only she hadn't given way to that sudden panic up by that bedroom window – or have staved it off just long enough to note the car's number . . .

She was in the Hobbs's hall now, by the phone. It was a very modern phone, typical of Alec, with a push-button arrangement instead of a dial. She wasn't used to it, and fumbled desperately with the buttons for several seconds before getting through to the Scotland Yard switchboard.

The black Capri could be half a mile away by now; perhaps a whole mile, even two . . .

When the switchboard operator answered, she was on the point of giving Gideon's extension number. But Alec was the father, after all – he ought to know first. So she asked to be put through to the Assistant Commissioner (Crime).

A bad mistake. She found herself talking to the newly-engaged secretary, who didn't know her, didn't know anything about Penny or the baby, and didn't even know how to recognise urgency in a voice when she heard it.

"I am sorry, but the Assistant Commissioner is in conference, and cannot be disturbed."

"Well, the moment he can," said Kate, chokingly, "tell – tell him his baby son's been kidnapped – "

"*What?*"

The secretary's startled yelp still ringing in her ears, Kate slammed down the receiver, then picked it up again and redialled the Scotland Yard number. That was the quickest way to get back to the switchboard, though there wasn't much that was quick about the way her fingers, wet with perspiration, slipped and slithered over those stupid push buttons.

The black Capri could now be four, five miles away. Past Wimbledon, if it was heading south. Near Vauxhall, if it was making for central London . . .

She gave the switchboard Gideon's number. The ringing tone seemed to go on for an eternity – an eternity during which the hall seemed to whirl round her, faster and faster, like the blurring spokes on the wheels of that pram.

Her heart . . . The doctors had warned her about it, years ago. Surely it wasn't going – wasn't going – to –

Everything began to go dark and she felt herself swaying, but just managed to keep on her feet by gripping hold of the wooden ledge on which the telephone stood. She had to do that with her left hand. Her right was still holding on to the receiver. Not that that was much good, she thought stupidly. There was such a ringing in her ears that she doubted if she could hear George, even if he did come on the phone.

Next moment, she realised that that was an exaggeration.

Through the ringing, as if from a great, immeasurable distance, came a familiar grunt.

"Gideon here."

Relief at hearing that familiar voice started tears welling again in Kate's eyes. Everything would be all right, she told herself, now that she'd got through to George.

All she had to do was tell him – tell him –

Summoning up all her strength, she somehow forced herself to speak, but to her depthless horror, found that she could not force any sense into her words.

"Hurry, love. The black Capri. Ten, twelve miles away," she said, and managed one more word – "baby" – before she fell, unconscious, to the floor.

At the other end of the line, it was Gideon's turn to know many kinds of fear.

7   Crisis

The next few minutes were, in fact, amongst the most anxious that Gideon had ever known.

"Kate!" he shouted. "Kate, love . . . *Kate* . . ."

There was silence on the line, a silence so complete that it was terrifying. But there was no silence inside Gideon's head, where Kate's words were repeating themselves endlessly.

"*Hurry, love. The black Capri. Ten, twelve miles away, Baby . . .*"

His mind flew back to his last telephone conversation with Kate, just five minutes before. She had been excitedly burbling on about the baby George in the pram at the end of the lawn. Then – with his encouragement – she had been going upstairs to indulge her whim about putting on a swimsuit.

If a kidnapping gang had been waiting to snatch the baby, that would have given them the perfect opportunity. Kate must have realised what was happening a shade too late, and come rushing downstairs – probably to see the pram empty, and the car – this black Capri – driving off.

What could have happened then?

She must have dashed indoors to ring him or Alec, and there must have been some delay. Why otherwise would the car now be "ten, twelve miles away?" And the strain of the whole thing – witnessing the snatch, and then battling with a frustrating delay – had told on Kate's heart, which had not been strong for years.

Had she fainted – or had an attack – or . . .

Gideon was gripping the receiver so hard that it seemed as if its plastic stem would crack at any moment. It was almost as though he was willing it to produce some sign of life: a breath, a groan, a gasp, even a rustle would do.

Suddenly, as if in response to his will, the silence was broken – but only by an infuriating clicking, indicating that somebody was desperately trying to come through on that line. Whoever it was evidently decided to try another route. The clicking stopped, and instantly, the second of the three phones on Gideon's desk shrilled. Gideon picked up its receiver with his other hand.

"Gideon," he barked, so impatiently that the word came out as a single syllable.

"George." It was Alec, an Alec whose voice was hard to recognise at first. All his poise and polish was gone, so was that new-found ring of command. He sounded almost like a dazed, stunned child. "George, Kate's been trying to reach me, but I'm in a conference here with Sir Reginald, and my secretary wouldn't put her through. She left a strange message – about the baby being kidnapped. I thought she might have gone on to ring you. Have you heard from her?"

"Yes, I've heard from her," Gideon snapped, and added hoarsely: "Just."

"Just?"

"Yes. She was starting to tell *me* something about the baby - but couldn't get it out. And now I think she's fainted." Gideon's voice broke. "Please God, it *is* only a faint . . . " He cleared his throat, and recovered himself rapidly. "Listen, Alec. I think she must be lying right by the phone, in your hall. Isn't there a neighbour you can ring - someone who can get over there straight away?"

"Yes," said Alec promptly. "Miss Thompson at number twenty-three. She's just the person, because she's a retired nurse. I'll ring her now."

"How can she get in? Has she a key?"

"No. But the garden door should be open, the one leading from the lounge on to the lawn. If it isn't, I'll tell her to smash the glass . . . George?"

"Yes?"

"About the baby. Could you get anything out of what Kate said?"

"It's only a guess," said Gideon, "but I think she was telling me that he's been taken by some people in a black Ford Capri, and is - or was when she phoned, about a minute ago - ten to twelve miles away."

"Oh, my God," Alec whispered, then suddenly he was shouting. "Christ, I must get things moving."

"Leave that to me," said Gideon softly, desperately. "At least until you've got Miss Thompson moving."

"Oh, of course. Sorry, George. Hold on. I'll do it right away."

Alec did not hang up, but went off to ring his neighbour on another phone. For a crazy moment, Gideon found himself holding one receiver in each hand, both of them silent. Yet he did not wish to return either of them to its rest. The one in his right hand was his direct link with the Hobbs's hall, with Kate. If she gave the slightest sound, no matter how far away her mouth was from the phone, he somehow knew he would hear . . . The receiver in his left hand was linked with Scott-Marle's office: Alec had said "I'm at a conference *here* with Sir Reginald." Nothing would save more time in getting the search for the baby started than if the Chief Commissioner himself took charge. Perhaps, if he shouted loud enough, Scott-Marle himself might hear and pick up the phone.

"Sir Reginald!" Gideon bellowed, loud enough to turn the receiver in that distant office into a miniature amplifier.

For several long seconds there was no reply, and Gideon, in a mood of savage desperation, was tempted to slam down both receivers after all. What was the point of standing here like a dummy, sickened to the heart and soul by silence, silence, silence . . .

Suddenly the receiver in his left hand sprang to life. He raised it to his ear.

"There was no need to shout, George," came the voice of Sir Reginald. "I'm not deaf – unless, that is, you've just made me so! As it happens, I heard your whole conversation with Alec on the desk loudspeaker, and have just been giving instructions to Uniform to start an all-area search for the black Ford Capri." There was a slight pause. Then he added: "I have done something else, too – ordered a car with motor-cycle escort to proceed at full speed, breaking all limits, to Alec's house. I suggest you and Alec go in it. Neither of you should be here when your hearts and minds are there . . . Oh, and give me the name of Kate's doctor. I'll see that he is rushed there too."

69

In a very different way, Scott-Marle's voice had become as hard to recognise as Alec's. The usually calm and controlled Sir Reginald was talking in a succession of nervous spurts, betraying an intense concern. Gideon was dazed, almost awed. He had long realised that Scott-Marle, whatever his faults, was a dedicated policeman. But he had never encountered this emotional side of him before. It was almost as if he was making this crisis in the lives of his two top men his own.

"One other thing, George," he went on. "Obviously neither you nor Alec should take personal command in this case, even though you may both be tempted to. You are too emotionally involved; it would be like asking a surgeon to operate on himself! So I suggest you take a good Chief Detective Superintendent with you - say, Honiwell. He handled the Cargill kidnapping case brilliantly some years ago - "

Gideon did not hear another word.

Everything coming through his left ear had been faded out by the faint sound that was reaching him through his right . . . and the deafening beating of his heart that it caused.

"*George. Hurry, George. The . . . the baby . . .*"

It was a distant, echoing, incoherent murmur, but it was unmistakably Kate - Kate talking to herself as she returned to consciousness on the floor of the Hobbs's hall.

There were other sounds now, too.

A door crashing open . . . brisk, professional, nurse-like footsteps . . . and an obviously hospital-trained voice saying:

"Good morning, Mrs. Gideon. How are you feeling? You *have* had a nasty fall, haven't you . . . Just sip this."

Then there was a click, and the line went dead. Clearly the

tidy-minded Miss Thompson, in bending to examine Kate, had noticed the dangling receiver behind her and automatically hung up.

It didn't matter. The important thing was that Kate was alive, and if not well, at least returning to consciousness.

If he hurried, and if that dash in the police car was as dramatically fast as Scott-Marle planned, it was even possible that he might be by her side within a few minutes of her coming to.

He was about to charge towards the door when suddenly he became aware of a furious clicking in his other ear – and then of Scott-Marle barking:

"George, are you there? The car's waiting, and Alec's already gone down to it. What's the matter with you, man? Are you all right?"

"Perfectly all right, sir," said Gideon. "And I'm coming now. It's just that – "

He sought for a phrase to describe what had happened, and suddenly hit on the right one.

" —— I was urgently wanted on another phone."

*　　*　　*

It seemed that Alec had been giving orders as well as Scott-Marle, and with the personal directives of both the Chief Commissioner and the Assistant Commissioner behind it, what finally left for the Hobbs's house resembled a presidential motorcade.

First came two motorcyclists and a police car with its sirens wailing at full blast. Then came Gideon and Hobbs, in the back seat of Scott-Marle's official Bentley – a car which carried the crest of the Metropolitan Police Force emblazoned on its doors. This was followed by an area car containing Chief

71

Detective Superintendent Matt Honiwell, with a detective sergeant and two constables; and bringing up the rear were two police Pandas loaded with forensic experts – fingerprint men, photographers, the inevitable video operator (for scene of the crime simulations, Gideon supposed) and also specialists in telecommunications and sound.

"If the kidnappers telephone a ransom demand," Hobbs told Gideon, shouting above the continuous blare of the sirens, "we've the means now to trace the call in fifteen seconds – less than a quarter of the usual time. And the speaker's voice will be not only recorded but computer-analysed . . . achieving a kind of Identikit on sound . . ."

Gideon tried hard to look impressed. He knew how desperately Alec needed to believe in his gimmickry at that moment. It was hardly the time to point out that he knew of no kidnapping case where such techniques had helped the inquiry at all.

They were out of central London now, heading south down roads which Gideon knew like the back of his hand, but which became strangely unfamiliar when hurtled down at 80 m.p.h., with roaring motorbikes and wailing sirens combining to make a raucous crescendo of sound. Along every street, in every shop doorway and almost, it seemed, at every window, there were faces turned towards them in startled, staring disbelief. A couple of schoolgirls actually waved handkerchiefs at them and cheered. They probably thought that he was a visiting prime minister, Gideon thought, not realising that his own face was as well known as any politician's, and that the word that was going round was that some big criminal gang was about to be rounded up – so big that George Gideon was taking on the job himself.

Despite one awkward hold-up halfway down the King's

Road, the motorcade arrived at Hurlingham in the incredible time of eleven minutes. Gideon grabbed the front doorkey from Alec's hand, and was first out of the car. Miss Thompson, a tall, grey-haired woman who looked every bit as professional at nursing as she had sounded on the phone, was waiting for him in the hall.

"Commander Gideon? Good afternoon. Your wife seems very much better, but I have persuaded her to lie down until the doctor comes. She is in one of the bedrooms upstairs - the spare one, I understand . . ."

Gideon went up there immediately. Kate looked very white and anxious, but otherwise not too bad. There was an empty teacup in a saucer beside the bed, and a plate with half a biscuit on it. It was good that she'd been eating and drinking.

"Hullo, love," said Gideon gently.

She managed a half-smile; but then it vanished.

"The baby," she said. "Is there any news about the – "

"Not so far," Gideon told her. "There hardly could be, yet. But we've a search for a black Ford Capri going on all over London, and downstairs Alec's got more policemen on the case than there are in Bow Street and Cannon Row put together. So don't worry. Just concentrate on telling me exactly what happened here . . ."

Kate told her story clearly, but haltingly.

She was still furious with herself for not having noted the number of the Ford. But during those few seconds by the bedroom window, she had had so many confusing impressions all at once. She mentioned the shadowy figure in the case, and her momentary feeling that he had looked familiar. But that was ridiculous, of course. She had only caught the merest glimpse of him, and wasn't even sure if there had been anyone there at all.

73

Gideon was dying to probe more deeply, and in any other circumstances, would have done. But Kate was becoming more anxious and agitated every second, and the only way he could think of to calm her down was to let her finish her story as soon as possible.

There were no surprises for him in the rest of it; just a new realisation of how horrible that moment had been when Kate had rushed into the garden and seen the pram overturned and empty.

At the end, struggling to sit up, Kate said, "Has Penny been told yet?"

"Alec's been trying to get through to her," Gideon told her. "But it's the recording studio's lunch break – and you know what Penny is for going off to the shops at the slightest opportunity!"

"Oh, George. She'll be in a dreadful state when she hears."

There was no denying that, and Gideon didn't try.

"There's one thing to thank God for, at any rate," he said. "George is being bottle-fed. Whoever the kidnappers are, they should be able to cope with that."

"But supposing they get the wrong mixture . . . or aren't careful about hygiene – or – "

Gideon was extremely relieved when, at that moment, the doctor arrived – a very flustered doctor, who had never been rushed to a case by police car before.

After examining Kate, he said that her pulse was good, and that she should make a complete recovery.

"I've given her an injection, and she'll sleep for seven to eight hours. When she wakes up, she *must* be kept away from anything that might cause stress or strain."

Gideon thanked him and saw him out, fighting the grim,

chilling feeling that he had been given an impossible task.

Until the baby was returned, every waking moment of Kate's life – and his, and Alec's, and Penny's, and Honiwell's – was liable to be *loaded* with stress and strain.

8   Brink

At least, thought Gideon, there was one thing to be thankful
for: Kate's moments for the next eight hours were going to
be sleeping, not waking, ones. He returned to the bedroom,
and stayed with her until the sedative had taken effect, and she
was fast asleep.

He kissed her gently on the forehead, crept out of the room,
and went back downstairs - to find Alec having a heated
discussion with Matt Honiwell in the hall. The expressions of
both men showed plainly that he had not been exaggerating
about the stress and strain. Alec's handsome but normally
rather wooden features looked grave and stern - grim enough
to have been carved in granite. Matt, one of the shrewdest
men at the Yard but also one of the most sensitive, had a
tousled, unkempt look, as though he'd been running a hand
too often through his thick mop of curly brown hair. That
hair, combined with his ready, sympathetic smile, gave Matt a

mild, almost cuddly air. It was difficult to believe that, in his time, he had taken on – and seen off – harder villains than almost anyone at the Yard.

As soon as he saw Gideon, Alec turned to him. "George, I've at last succeeded in reaching Penny at the recording studio – and I'm afraid she's taken the news very hard. In fact, she sounded almost hysterical and is obviously in no fit state to drive. My own car's still at the Yard, of course, and so I'm sending a police car round to pick her up and bring her here. It sounds bloody cold and impersonal, I know, and I desperately wanted to be in that car. But Matt won't allow me out of the house, in case the kidnappers ring. Couldn't *you* take the call if they do?"

Gideon hesitated. It was unusual, to say the least, for a Chief Detective Superintendent to put his foot down with an Assistant Commissioner. Just one more proof, he thought, of the strength that lay hidden behind Matt's cuddly exterior.

"Matt's in charge today, not you or me," he reminded Alec. "And he wouldn't be much good to either of us if he was the kind to accept back-seat driving on the case."

Matt flashed him a grateful smile. "I'm not being awkward for the sake of it, George, believe me."

"I know you're not," Gideon said. "Kidnappers have a nasty habit of ringing off if they find they can't talk direct to the person they want – and in this case, that's liable to be the father, not the grandfather, of the child."

Matt's smile vanished. Yet again, he ran a hand through his hair.

"Nothing must be allowed to mess up that call. Because at the moment, it looks like our one and only hope of getting a positive lead."

Alec's temper flared again – a sure sign of the mental turmoil he was in. Normally there was no one more self-possessed, whatever the emergency. But who could say what was normal behaviour for a copper chasing the kidnappers of his own son? His own *newborn* son.

"Are you telling me that you and all these men have failed to discover *anything* so far?"

It was a ridiculously unfair question to ask a detective who had barely been on the case for an hour. Matt, typically, took no offence, but just sorrowfully recited the long succession of blanks that he and his men had drawn since arriving at the house. No fingerprints had been detected on any part of the upturned pram. No trace of footprints had been discovered, even after the most exhaustive search of the lawn and the adjacent flowerbeds. Not the faintest suggestion of a tyre-track had been found on the sun-baked strip of road outside the garden gate. Although two detective sergeants had been knocking at doors all down the street, they had not found an eye-witness to any part of the incident – not even an *ear* witness to such sounds as car doors slamming or the baby crying. Nor had there been any results from Scott-Marle's all-area search for the suspect car. The trouble there was, of course, the time lag between Kate's discovery of the kidnapping and getting anyone to listen to her at the Yard. By the time the first alarm had been raised, the car could have been virtually anywhere in Greater London, Kent or Surrey.

By the end of the recital, Alec was looking no longer angry, but deflated and despairing.

Honiwell – rarely a failure when it came to dealing with people – immediately hit on a way to lift his spirits.

"At least, thanks to your technicians, we are equipped to

get the most from the kidnapper's call, when it comes," he said.

Alec brightened. Just for a second, he became once again the New Broom of the C.I.D., ushering in an era of new techniques.

"They've certainly worked miracles in a short time," he said, and turned to Gideon. "Have you seen what they've set up in the living room, George? If not, step this way . . ."

Gideon and Matt followed Alec into the living room; and even Gideon, distrustful as he was of gadgetry for its own sake, was impressed by what he saw. The room now resembled nothing so much as a broadcasting studio. The elegant furniture - from a wall-unit with concealed lighting to Penny's baby grand - had all been moved into a single corner to allow room for a complex network of amplifiers, tape recorders, portable computers and control panels, spread out across a good third of the thick, deep blue carpet. In a central clearing stood a mahogany desk with a comfortable leather chair behind it, both imported from Alec's study across the hall. On the desk was a microphone, with a pair of headphones beside it, and a red light waiting to be flashed on. On either side of the desk, technicians wearing headphones were kneeling in front of hastily rigged-up panels with so many dials, knobs and switches that they looked as though they belonged in the pilot's cabin of the Concorde. Close to the door nine or ten chairs had been drawn up in two rows, with headphones waiting on the seat of every chair.

"From now onwards," Alec explained, "every call coming to the telephone in the hall will be switched through here. When the phone rings in the hall, the red light will flash on, and obviously I'll go to the desk, put on the headphones, and take the call from there. Every word of it will be recorded, magnified and analysed by a dozen different computer processes, while the conversation is actually going on. And – '' he indicated the chairs ''– we've an audience area so that you, Matt, and everyone else involved with the inquiry can listen in.''

''On the theory, I suppose,'' said Gideon, ''that half a dozen pairs of ears are better than one.''

''Half a dozen!'' Alec laughed. ''This equipment is equal to a hundred pairs of ears, each a thousand times superior to a human one. The moment the kidnapper speaks, we'll have a computer voice-print as personal as a fingerprint. And no matter how the voice is disguised, we'll have a positive reading on sex and age. That's only the start. Every background noise will be magnified. If someone stands on, say, bare, creaking floorboards, we'll know it's an empty house. If a heavy lorry goes by outside, we'll know it's near a main road – ''

Hobbs went on and on, but Gideon was no longer listening. A thought had struck him that was so painful, it blotted out everything else, like a vast nuclear mushroom cloud blacking out the sun.

Hobbs and Matt were staking everything on getting clues, or a lead, from the ransom call.

But the odds were almost a thousand to one against there being one.

If the baby George's kidnappers had been after ransom money, surely the very last victim they'd have chosen would be the son of the Assistant Commissioner of Scotland Yard – and the grandson of the C.I.D.'s Commander!

It was very much more likely that the motive was revenge – and that they were up against one or more of the countless villains whom Alec or he had brought to book over their long years of fighting crime.

Worse conclusions followed from there – some of them so terrible that Gideon's brain couldn't bring itself to put them into words.

If revenge was the motive, the kidnappers would have no reason for calling – except to sneer or jeer, and these days, they could do that at far more length and with far less risk by just sending a taped message through the post.

A phone call from the kidnappers was, then, not only unlikely, but something to be dreaded if, by any chance, it did come. It would mean that they were dealing with a dangerously twisted mind. And the call would probably be just to say where the baby's body could be . . .

With a violent effort of will, Gideon forced that thought out of his mind. It was almost as difficult as tearing a strangling hand away from his throat, but at that moment there came an interruption.

The telephone rang.

*   *   *

It rang out in the hall, but there were instant repercussions in the studio-like living room. The red light flashed on the microphone desk. The kneeling technicians stiffened and began frenziedly turning knobs and checking dials. Alec, looking eager and excited now that the waiting was over, strode purposefully across to the desk, sat down behind it, and donned the headphones. Gideon waited, battling with a depthless sense of dread.

"Hullo. Hobbs speaking," Alec said.

Then, his eagerness gone, replaced by a look of extreme tension, he turned to Gideon.

81

"I told the Yard switchboard to stop all calls here, except in a case of extreme emergency. But apparently this is one – or what claims to be one. It's Lemaitre, George. From Whitgate. For you."

Gideon crossed to the desk, took over the headphones from Alec, and said very coldly into the mike:

"Yes, Lem? Keep it short, for Chrissake. No wild conclusions, please – just facts."

"Will these do to be getting on with?" said a grim and bitter Lemaitre. "Reports of *five* random shootings have come in from different parts of Whitgate in the past quarter of an hour. Three dead, two wounded, and a constable, poor old Charlie Morton, in intensive care, with a bullet an inch from his heart. *Now* do you suppose the new top brass will believe that this place is on the brink of a bloodbath?"

Lemaitre's angry Cockney splutter was making the dials on the control panels jump as if they were registering a seismic explosion.

Still totally unaware that every word was being listened to, taped, dissected and computer-analysed in the presence of the "new top brass" himself, Lem rushed on:

"Not that it matters a lot, really. We might have stopped it between us this morning, George. I can't see anyone stopping it now."

*　　　*　　　*

In all his career, Gideon had never been allowed to concentrate his whole attention on one case at a time, not even on one crisis at a time. Long experience had taught him how to divide his mind into watertight compartments, and this stood him in good stead now, even though this time the pressure of worry was so great that at any moment he felt that one of those compartments might spring a leak.

Normally he only had to switch his thoughts on to a case, for all the relevant details to spring instantly into his mind, like the soldiers of a crack regiment assembling on parade. This time, he had to struggle for several seconds, as if through a thick fog, before he could remember even the salient facts. Out of the fog, the baby George's face seemed to stare at him, with that famous Gideon glare. Would he – would anyone – ever see it again?

He closed his eyes for a moment, in a Herculean effort to pull himself together. The baby's face vanished, and the whole Whitgate situation spread itself in front of him, a grim panorama of political fanaticism, despairing youth, mindless hate and potential violence, and, if Lem was right, a time bomb set to explode that very night into London's first open street war.

Was Lem right?

Could two or three mentally subnormal pot-shooters, killing random victims in isolated incidents, really unleash the necessary torrents of political hate? In other words, however much they might be spoiling for a fight, would the followers of Jeremy Caxton and Sir Gilbert Fordyce really start firing at each other simply because "killing for thrills" had become a local habit?

It was possible. Anything was possible in this strange era of pointless violence and motiveless murder. But Gideon still doubted it. Once again, he had a nagging feeling that there was an unknown factor in the case; that the man who had been slipping guns into the hands of those sick weirdos in the cinema had a deeper and more mysterious purpose than starting street fights.

But what could that purpose possibly be?

Gideon had to admit that he could not even begin to hazard a guess.

One thing was certain. This was a time, not for theories, but for action. And it had to be action on a big scale. Nothing else could effectively halt the killings now.

Instinctively, Gideon began barking commands into the microphone.

"Listen, Lem. Stop panicking and get cracking. First, I suggest you get that cinema to suspend all showings of *They Kill for Thrills* until further notice, on police instructions."

"Will do, Gee Gee."

"But don't let the cinema announce the closure. I want officers at the door, taking the names of everyone who comes to see that film for the rest of the day – and searching any of them who look remotely suspicious. There's just a chance that the man who hands out these guns doesn't realise yet that he's been rumbled. In which case, you'll catch him, with maybe two or three guns on him. Have Detective-Sergeant Baker – that is the name of the man who had the strange close encounter in the cinema, isn't it? – have him on stand-by in the foyer; he ought to be able to identify the gun merchant on sight."

"Will do," said Lem again. "But all that's closing the stable door after the horse has bolted, if you ask me. The gun merchant's done *his* job. The problem is how to stop his loony customers doing theirs." His voice rose to almost a hysterical pitch. "I hate to say it, but there could be one of them walking now down any street in Whitgate, or hiding behind any door. And no one's safe, Gee Gee, literally no one. The three hit just now were a milkman's assistant, from behind a wall when he was delivering the last pint of the morning, an estate agent getting into his car in the High Street, and a bus conductor leaving the garage for lunch. The two wounded were a couple of old age pensioners – "

"Right," Gideon interrupted. "This means area patrolling on a scale we haven't used since the Wellesley Estate Case. We need to have area cars covering every street in Whitgate every five to ten minutes throughout the day. Backing that, we must start a major C.I.D. operation throughout the area. You've already questioned the cinema staff, haven't you? Now we must begin questioning doctors, hospitals, schools, youth leaders, community centres, disco operators – anyone or anything which might help us to build up a check-list of potential gun-toters. After all, Lem, these pot-shooters *are* a recognisable type. They were given the guns precisely *because* they were recognised for what they were – even in the darkness of a cinema! If our men can get to recognise them too . . . "

"You mean arrest every vicious-looking yobbo on sight?" said Lem. "You'd end up putting half the teenage population of Whitgate inside."

"I'd sooner do that," said Gideon grimly, "than have half the adult population dead! Which reminds me – we must implement the other measures that I was suggesting this morning. We must involve Special Branch; have a house to house search for guns in the key trouble-spots; arrange for at least a hundred men from Uniform to be there at those political meetings tonight . . . and for most of them to be armed."

"Aren't you forgetting something?" asked Lem sagely. "A lot of that was vetoed this morning – I suspect by the new A.C. Are you sure he'll withdraw his bloody veto now? It's going to be hard for him to eat his words before the end of his first day.''

It was a painful moment.

Gideon stared across the room at Alec, who was sitting, alone, on one of the chairs in what he had called the ''audience section''. His headphones were on; he had obviously heard every word, but his face was expressionless. Remembering his outbursts of temper with the sympathetic Matt, Gideon dreaded to hear his reactions to the recklessly impertinent Lem. He might even be bitter about the way he, Gideon, had forgotten the veto and proposed all the disputed measures again.

The moment dragged on, with Alec still silent, his face still registering no emotion at all.

Then, quietly and with a faint, wry smile, he said, ''Not for the first time by a long, long way, it looks as though you were right, George, and I was wrong. Please take it that the – er – bloody veto is withdrawn.'' He was very much the old Alec Hobbs now, the quiet, efficient Deputy Commander. ''May I suggest the best way of getting the whole package of proposals implemented is to dictate them to Barnaby, and get him to present them to Scott-Marle as a joint submission from you and me. He will contact Special Branch and give the orders to Uniform. Meanwhile, Barnaby himself can see that Lem gets the extra C.I.D. men he needs, by transferring them from other areas.'' Before Gideon could thank him, Hobbs had changed again – into a desperately anxious father. ''But George . . . could you possibly do it on another phone? The Post Office will be here installing extra lines in a few minutes, but until they do . . . ''

Gideon nodded.

''It's all being laid on, Lem,'' he said into the microphone.

"I've got to go now. Good luck."

He "hung up" by the unusual method of pressing a switch beside the mike. Then he put down the headphones and hurried out, leaving Alec, Matt and the technicians to begin their long wait for a call which, he still privately believed, was very unlikely to come.

Miss Thompson was in the hall, just leaving. She was looking flushed and excited at her encounter with high police drama, and brushed aside Gideon's profuse thanks for all her help. "A pleasure, Commander, and I'm so glad your wife is on the road to recovery . . . Yes, of course I'd be delighted to let you use my phone . . . "

In a minute, he was in the retired nurse's hall – smart, neat but drab after the *Homes and Gardens* elegance of the Hobbs's.

He rang the Yard, and was put through to Barnaby. He expected him to sound tired and harassed. On his first day as Acting Deputy Commander, he was really having to deputise for him, in the fullest sense of the term. The afternoon had already brought five shootings, including three murders, and now he was being asked to deal personally with Scott-Marle. But Barnaby's voice sounded as unflustered and unemotional as ever. There was one moment when it held a hint of undisguised satisfaction.

"I take it, sir, that you want me to direct all possible C.I.D. men from neighbouring areas to Whitgate?"

"That's right," said Gideon. "Though Honiwell may want a few to help him here. You'll have to ask him about that, not me."

"That will mean taking men from areas like Pimlico."

"It will."

"And closing down all wasteful projects . . . such as the one I drew your attention to this morning."

Gideon smiled faintly. All right, you bastard, he thought, you've got me.

Aloud he said, briskly, "You're quite right, Barnaby. Tell Price to close his Swanleigh stake-out – now."

9   No Protection

It took Derek Price all of thirty seconds to stammer out one short sentence to Anne Swanleigh and her father Reggie. Even when he'd got the sentence out, he was ashamed of it. It had sounded as stilted as a passage from a police report.

"I'm - I'm afraid that it's been decided to - er - to discontinue the surveillance on - on - this shop - with - with - immediate effect."

They both stared at him as though stunned. Price's large, pugnacious face turned a brick red; he looked ridiculously like a young farmer, about to wave a stick at some trespasser. But on Price, embarrassment often had the reverse effect from the expected one, and tended to loosen, rather than tie, his tongue. Suddenly he was no longer a policeman stumbling over jargon; he was a close friend of the family blurting out confidences.

"It's that b-bloody new Deputy Commander, Paul Barnaby. He was on at me first thing this morning to close

89

that stake-out. He's on a cost-efficiency drive, and I think he'd heard stories that I was only keeping it going as a personal favour. I saw G-Gideon himself and got Barnaby overruled. But since then, two big emergencies have come up. Somebody at the Yard has pressed the panic button – and Barnaby is sending every C.I.D. man for miles around to one place or the other. I've been ordered to drop everything I'm doing, and go to Whitgate. My Detective Sergeant, Potter, is off to help with a kidnapping inquiry at Fulham. I'm not even allowed to put a uniformed constable outside here. They're all wanted at Whitgate for special area patrols. I'll s-still be on call, of course, in any emergency. I'll leave you my Whitgate number – and I reckon that I can be over here from there in five minutes if – if – "

He broke off, abruptly, knowing only too well what they were thinking. Murdering attackers don't give you much time to ring up police stations – and kill in seconds, not minutes . . .

They were all in the little back room behind the shop. The shop itself was still closed for lunch, even though it was, in fact, a good half hour past its 2.15 p.m. reopening time. Anne was still in the process of giving her father his lunch: a pitifully sad spectacle because each forkful of food had to be put into his mouth as though he were a baby. Occasionally he would raise a hand a few inches, just enough to guide her arm: an indication that the paralysis wasn't quite complete.

He had made no movement, though, since Price's shattering announcement. Neither, for that matter, had Anne. They were like figures in a tableau. Even a forkful of sausage was suspended in midair, halfway to Reggie's mouth.

Price kept talking, or rather, spluttering.

"Of course, as soon as I'm – I'm off duty, I'll be round as

usual. But not knowing how the Whitgate situation will develop, I'm afraid I can't say what time that'll be tonight.''

Anne put the fork down on a plate. The bit of sausage on it was cold and congealing.

''You know you'll be welcome, whatever time it is,'' she said, adding, with a hurried glance at her father: ''Er – as long as it's not halfway through the night . . . ''

A surreptitious wink (startling on that rather prim face) indicated that, in reality, there would be no objections to a small-hours visit at all.

Reggie said nothing, but there was a strange glittering look in his eye. Did he suspect that Price's frequent evening calls on his daughter were supplemented by even more frequent late-night visits to her bedroom? There were times when Price thought he did, and bitterly disapproved. But he never said a word about it. After all, the poor old boy was in no position to complain. Anne had given up a great deal to come home and look after him, and God knew what a strain on her nerves it had been to keep on serving in that shop, day after day. Added to that, she was hardly able to leave the house even at night, because her father was too helpless to be alone, and her only help in caring for him came from a district nurse whom he, Price, had arranged to call for a couple of hours every afternoon. With Anne doing so much for him, Reggie would have been very ungrateful if he had started getting nosey or disapproving about her love life!

Nevertheless, Price *was* somehow surprised that Swanleigh had never attempted to play the heavy father. Perhaps that was because he so looked the part. He had a thin face with high cheekbones, and this, coupled with straggly grey hair and large, staring eyes, gave him an appearance that any Victorian tragedian might have envied. It was hard to believe that he

91

had looked like that in his days as a maths teacher. No one would ever have called him "Reggie" if he had. It was as though the melodramatically tragic events that had befallen him since had turned him into a melodramatic figure, with a compulsion to heighten the drama and tension all around him, all the time. No wonder Anne's nerves were constantly on edge, Price thought. He really believed that but for his presence, and their clandestine affair, the poor darling would have been round the twist by now. Thank God an end to her living nightmare was at last in sight. If only he could get them through the next few days without the unthinkable happening, she'd be back in training college, her father would be at his sister's, and the shop, with all its horrific memories, would be closed for good.

His own life would be emptier and lonelier without Anne around, of course . . . but the college wasn't far away, and there'd be the long summer vacation soon. In any case, Anne only had a year to go now before she qualified. After that, provided that she could get a post in a school near London, they'd made plans about taking a flat together, perhaps getting married. The old boy presented grave problems, though. Anne would not hear of him going into a home, and they could not expect the sister to take care of him for ever. It looked as though he'd have to come and live with them, for at least half the year. Both for his sake and for Anne's, Price hated the prospect, but no other option seemed open. He also hated himself for thinking as coldly as this about it. If only, he thought for the thousandth time, he could bring himself to *like* Reggie, instead of just pitying him. But something – probably the shock of his wife's death – seemed to have paralysed the old boy's ability to feel anything except nervous tension. It was almost as though he was no longer a human being, just an echo chamber endlessly reverberating with fear.

He had recovered from the shock announcement suffi-ciently to speak at last, and fixed Price with those large, staring eyes.

"You mean you're going to withdraw all police protection from this shop? After everything that's happened here? With the killer still at large?"

Price was compelled to stutter "yes", but added:

"You – you must remember, sir, that he last struck a long time ago."

"Thirteen weeks?" said Price. "What's thirteen weeks to a maniac with an obsession like this? Some killers remain quiescent for months . . . even years."

Price reddened. This was exactly the case he had put to Gideon that morning. But now, whatever his feelings, he had to argue against it, for the sake of calming the old boy's nerves.

"Such k-killers are pretty rare," he pointed out. "But if you're as worried as all that, why not close the shop – at any rate for a day? By tomorrow, the Whitgate business may be over . . . I may be able to go to Gideon again . . . "

"What's the use of closing the shop?" Swanleigh wailed. "*He* knows we're here. The doors, the windows – they're easy to break down with that claw hammer of his . . . " His eyes became wild, almost hysterical. "Anne saw something frightening only this morning, and it scared her so much that your man had to come across! How can you possibly say after that that we don't need protection now, more badly than ever?"

"Mr. Swanleigh," said Price. "Do you know all it was that terrified Anne?"

He went through the door leading into the shop. Picking

up one of the big rubber balls that Potter had described, he returned with it to the little back room. He was about to bounce it, but remembered just in time what Potter had told him about the effect that had on Anne. So he simply held the ball out, right under her father's nose.

"It was just *this*," he said. "Just this, bouncing on the floor. Nothing very hurtful in that, is there?"

"Yes. It was s-silly of me, wasn't it?" said Anne, her voice faltering.

Price glanced up at her sharply, and noticed that she had paled even at the sight of the ball. Suddenly an odd sound – something between a gasp and a choking groan – made him turn back to the invalid.

Reggie Swanleigh had gone not pale, but grey. His head was lolling forward on his chest, with a strand of his long, straggling hair actually touching the ball, and his staring eyes a bare three inches away from it.

Just for a moment, it was almost as if he could not see it, almost as if he had fainted dead away.

10   Assassin

By this time, Londoners in their millions were beginning to feel as unprotected as the Swanleighs.

The news about the pot-shot incidents at Whitgate had been on TV and the radio, and was making the main head-lines in the evening paper. Bracketed with it – fighting with it for headline space – was the story about the disappearance of the Hobbs baby.

The two news items together were enough to make the most complacent citizen feel uneasy. Six perfectly ordinary people quietly going about their business – a milkman, an estate agent, a bus conductor, two old age pensioners and a police constable – had been shot without the slightest warning, without the faintest rhyme or reason, apparently just for kicks. Three of them were dead, and three wounded – the police constable very gravely. It had all happened in broad daylight, within two miles of central London. And if anyone was still rash enough to think that the police could protect him from such things, look what had happened – in that very same hour – to the baby son of Scotland Yard's own Assistant Commissioner. It had been snatched from the pram while being watched over by its grandmother – the wife of Commander Gideon himself!

That last fact was, from the public's point of view, the most telling blow. Whenever there were any fears about crime getting out of hand, people automatically thought of Gideon and were somehow reassured. For more than two decades his face had been seen on the TV screens at almost every moment of crisis in the war against crime, bluntly spelling out the situation in terms that everyone could understand, and making promises of police action that were always promptly and punctiliously kept, with Gideon very often at the forefront of that action himself.

But this time, the tide of vicious lawlessness had risen so high that it was attacking and engulfing the great champion of the law himself! And at that thought, despite a phenomenal May temperature soaring into the highest eighties, almost all London shuddered.

Who could feel safe in any street if a harmless estate agent, walking down a busy high street at high noon, could be shot and killed?

Who could feel safe in his back garden if the Assistant Commissioner's own baby wasn't safe in *his*?

Who, in fact, could feel safe anywhere, literally, under the sun?

There was no panic on the surface of London life, but there were signs in plenty of great uneasiness underneath. There were far fewer baskers in the sunlight at London's parks than might have been expected on such a glorious day. When the five o'clock rush hour began, people for once really seemed to be rushing, looking as if they'd be thankful to get to their trains, buses or Underground stations – anywhere away from the open street.

In Whitgate itself, the fear in the air was as easy to feel as the scorching sun on one's face. Ever since lunch time, the High Street had been as devoid of shoppers as if it were a Sunday afternoon. Everywhere else in the Whitgate area, you could walk for hundreds of yards without encountering a single pedestrian. And in the trouble-spot districts, the few gangs of youths still on the streets walked quickly and nervously, in marked contrast to their usual truculent sauntering.

Yet although the tension continually mounted, the risk of getting fired at by a pot-shooter was actually lessening with every hour that passed.

Following Gideon's plan of action, Lemaitre had a very successful afternoon.

The operation at the Screen Scene cinema, where C.I.D. men had secretly suspended the showing of *They Killed for Thrills,* but stayed by the box office and stopped everyone who tried to buy tickets for the film, had produced startling results. They had not caught the gun distributor, but two obviously subnormal youths had turned up for the first performance of the afternoon, and a loaded revolver had been found on each. Obviously they had become as hooked on the film as though it were a drug, and could not let a day go by without getting their fix. Probably watching it with loaded guns in their pockets – actually in possession of the power to turn the film's fantasy into bloody reality – had given them a double thrill. One of them, a boy of eighteen with a mental age of around nine, was just a harmless fantasist: his revolver had never been fired and he hadn't even worked out how to disengage the safety catch. The other, a twenty-two-year-old tough with a long police record for drunkenness and vandalism, was a very different case. Four bullets had been discharged from his Smith and Wesson, and after an hour of questioning by Lemaitre at his most relentless, he had broken down and confessed to being responsible for the wounding of the two old age pensioners. It seemed almost incredible that he could have calmly strolled into a cinema within minutes of committing such a crime . . . until one thought of it in terms of a sick mind high on sick fantasy, and desperately needing to escape back into it with the least possible delay.

One thing that pleased Lemaitre was the thought that he had stuck to "the new top brass's f . . . . . g barmy rules", as he thought of them, and still come out winning. A video camera, with sound equipment, had been installed in the interrogation room at Whitgate, and had been switched on all through his questioning of the twenty-two-year-old. Lem found that it hadn't inhibited him half as much as he had expected. In fact, within five minutes, he had forgotten it was there. That meant, of course, that any Scotland Yard high-up monitoring the tape would find his knowledge of colourful Cockney dramatically increased. But what did that matter? Even the Paul Barnabys of this world had to learn, sooner or later, that you didn't get confessions out of murdering yobbos by saying "Tut, tut" and "Dear, dear".

The other police operations had been equally successful. The area-wide questioning of doctors, schoolteachers, youth leaders and others had produced a list of over fifty youths who were thought dim enough, or insane enough, to have welcomed the sudden secret gift of a loaded gun. A team of detectives – led, as a matter of fact, by the newly-arrived Chief Detective Superintendent Derek Price – had visited the homes

98

of twenty-six of them, with the gratifying result that five more pot-shooters had been tracked down. One – a frenetic sixteen-year-old – had been found by Price himself, hiding in an airing-cupboard. He went there to take refuge from the police, then developed instant claustrophobia and ended by screaming to be let out. A search of the cupboard had revealed a revolver stuffed into a pillowcase and then wedged between the wall and the hot-water tank. Three of the bullet chambers in the revolver were empty, and when questioned the boy admitted – almost proudly – that he'd fired three times in the crowded High Street. He had done it on a sudden hysterical impulse, without aiming at anything or anyone in particular, he said. But despite the hysteria, he had remembered about the safety catch – and whether he'd aimed at him or not, that estate agent had died . . .

The killer of the bus conductor had been caught, too – a coloured youth so wildly trigger-happy that he had taken a pot-shot from his bedroom window at a passing police car! Under questioning – again by the remorseless Lemaitre, in front of a video camera at the police station – he had also confessed to the shooting of the milkman's assistant from behind a neighbour's garden wall.

"Case closed" could be written, then, over almost all the pot-shot incidents. Eight of the gun distributor's customers were under arrest, and if, as seemed likely, the man had been operating in just the one small cinema, there surely couldn't be many more.

It was true that the youth who had shot Constable Morton was still at large. Lemaitre had spent a harrowing half hour at Whitgate War Memorial Hospital, talking to old Charlie in the intensive care unit. Although very weak, Charlie had proved as solid and dependable a cop as ever, and given such a detailed description of his assailant that Lemaitre could almost see him: a fair-haired youth of sixteen or seventeen, only five foot three inches tall, wearing blue jeans and a greasy T-shirt of the same colour, with a chalk-white face, as expressionless as a mask, and pale blue eyes that could blaze with hate. Nobody answering that descripton, or anything resembling it, had been amongst those interviewed or arrested. And that was worrying.

It was also true that the gun distributor himself was still at large – and that was even more worrying.

But at least, by evening, it was beginning to look as if the pot-shot terror was largely over; it even seemed as if the hundred extra uniformed men who had been ordered to Whitgate to police the political meetings might be wasting their time.

Lemaitre walked over to the window of the first-floor office that had been placed at his disposal at Whitgate police station. It overlooked the Civic Centre where, in just half an hour's time, the meetings in question were to be held. Jeremy Caxton's Workers Unity Wing had booked a small hall just to the left of the entrance, and Sir Gilbert Fordyce's Back to Great Britain lot were taking a rather larger hall about ten feet down a corridor to the right. Followers of both parties, then, would be using the same central doorway at precisely the same time, both when arriving at and when leaving their meetings. Lemaitre had arranged for uniformed constables to be virtually lining the steps up to that central doorway, and for a dozen more to be in the corridor beyond.

They had already taken up their positions, and looked slightly ridiculous – they were the only people on that side of the street, apart from a few leaving or arriving at Whitgate Underground station next door.

100

Lemaitre jumped to the conclusion that supporters of both factions had been so terrified of being shot at that they had decided to stay home.

It was a premature conclusion, as usual. Presently a procession of cars drew up, headed by a battered 1960s Volkswagen, from which Jeremy Caxton emerged to stand fearlessly on the pavement, smoking, of all things, a fat cigar. He was soon surrounded by an entourage of twenty or thirty youngish supporters, the men mostly bearded and bespectacled, the girls chiefly of the intense, Women's Lib type, wearing black sweaters and jeans.

A few minutes later Sir Gilbert Fordyce arrived, in a gleaming red Mercedes. A large pear-shaped man with a face that seemed permanently red with anger, he too remained on the pavement for a while, as if determined not to be outdone by his opponent's show of courage. A rather more sinister entourage surrounded him – a score or more of tough-looking youths with leather jackets who at first, or even second, sight bore a close resemblance to a Soho heavy mob.

Lemaitre tensed, expecting trouble. But nothing of the sort occurred. The two political enemies, standing a mere twenty yards from each other, behaved with almost parliamentary decorum. Jeremy Caxton waved his cigar at Sir Gilbert, and made some remark that Lemaitre couldn't hear. Fordyce actually smiled, and replied with a courteous, if ironic, bow. Then the two turned and started going up the thirty-odd steps to the Civic Centre, moving in unison, if not exactly side by side. Their supporters followed, apparently exchanging good-humoured jokes with each other – and with the police. Other supporters of both parties had turned up now. There were perhaps a hundred people on the pavement, or on the steps, making their way into the halls. And the whole atmosphere was so amiable that they might all have been going to the Last Night of the Proms, rather than meetings at which they would screech and yell for hangings, floggings, or revolutions . . .

Why had it happened? Was it the effect of the beautiful May sunset, which was making the whole scene look as if it was being viewed through rose-tinted spectacles? Or was it shared pride – that they had all been courageous enough to stand about on the pavement, and brave the pot-shot terror?

Lemaitre wasn't sure. He only knew that he felt an overwhelming sense of relief. A rare grin split his lean, angular face in two.

Of course, he told himself, that made his theories look like ruins that Cromwell had knocked about a bit . . . but maybe that served him right, for so recklessly predicting a bleeding civil war!

Suddenly his grin faded. He had happened to glance at the Underground station next to the Civic Centre, and he found himself staring at its roof. The station was a one-storey building and the roof – a flat expanse of white concrete – was in full view, because it was on precisely the same level as his window. Dominating it was a large circular Underground sign, a good twenty feet in diameter, which was brilliantly lit up at night. At the moment it was lit up almost equally spectacularly by the setting sun, which was catching the glass and metal of the sign and turning it a dazzling crimson.

Staring at it made Lem's eyes water, and so he couldn't be sure . . . but he thought he had glimpsed someone crouching behind that sign. Someone with a revolver . . .

*　　　*　　　*

Major Robert Strode, deputy leader of the Back to Great

Britain Movement, was very grateful for the dazzling evening sun. He was sheltered from it by the Underground sign behind which he was crouching, and so it would not affect his eyes or his aim. Yet, by turning the sign into a blinding disc of fire, it made certain that he would not be spotted by anyone glancing up from the street below . . . and would not be interfered with until he had carried out his purpose: the assassination of his enemy in such a way that he himself would never, for a moment, be suspected of the crime.

A slim, tall, unmistakably military man in his late fifties, Strode had been in British Intelligence before his retirement eight years ago. His long years with that service had not earned him the promotion he felt he deserved. It had left him, in fact, secretly famished by unfulfilled ambition, tortured by an unslaked thirst for power – but it had given him a clear and extraordinarily subtle mind, which was functioning at full strength now.

None of the policemen on the Civic Centre steps had so much as glanced in his direction. They wouldn't have seen anything if they had. As he had calculated, the big Underground sign concealed him completely. The brilliant sunset was just a bonus. The only danger had been the possibility of a search of the Underground roof, but the police were looking out for crazy pot-shooters, not thinking in terms of military marksmen aiming from above.

If they had only done their homework properly, as he had, they would have realised that the roof was an ideal vantage-point, even for a pot-shooter. Being only one storey off the ground, it was well within revolver range of anyone using the main entrance to the Civic Centre. And there was not only good cover, there was even a quick and effective means of retreat. After the shooting, all he had to do was run a couple of yards and negotiate a drop of about ten feet into a side alley. The alley happened to be a cul-de-sac, but that didn't matter to Strode. He was not intending to hurry away from the scene.

As long as no one saw him actually jump down from the roof – and he planned to do that very quickly, within a second of the last shot being fired, and while the confusion was at its height – no one in a million years would imagine that he had been the killer.

He would stride on to the scene, appalled and aghast at the tragedy, roaring contempt at the ineptness of the police, and demanding public hangings for the filthy scum who killed and maimed the innocent for kicks . . .

It would make a fine inaugural speech for his first moments as the new leader of the Back to Great Britain Movement.

Yes – the new leader . . . for Strode's enemy was not his political opponent, Jeremy Caxton, but the man whose powerful presence blocked his personal road to power.

Coldly mastering the excitement which was making his arm tremble – that long-denied ambition being near to fulfilment at last – Strode raised his revolver and took careful aim.

His first shot left Sir Gilbert Fordyce sprawling on the steps, a bullet neatly drilled through his forehead.

*　　*　　*

It was the culmination of one of the most devious plots in political history; a plot that had become subtler and more complex as it developed.

Strode had originally intended to carry out his assassination so that suspicion fell on the Workers Unity Wing; but that would have meant a shoot-out between the two parties, both of which had formed action cells and acquired secret stores of guns and ammunition. Strode had heard that the Workers Unity Wing had recently been sent a consignment of guns by a Left-wing terrorist group, and it was plain bad tactics to plunge one's men into a war where they might be outgunned.

But suppose he could create a situation in which shots were being fired, pointlessly, for kicks, by yobbos all over Whitgate? Then it would seem that the death of Sir Gilbert was just a mindless incident, like the rest.

Strode had obtained a dozen or more Smith and Wessons, and a dozen clips of ammunition, from the secret BGBM armoury – an easy thing to do, as he happened to be in charge of it.

Then he had waited for the arrival at a Whitgate cinema of the cheap, made-for-ghouls film, *They Killed For Thrills*. The Major was rather addicted to films like that himself – especially, as a matter of fact, the ones with explicit rape scenes. He knew from experience how many dangerous-looking cranks were attracted to the cinema at every performance. At some shows (the early afternoon ones in particular) it was not uncommon to find as many as three or four weirdos banging about in their seats and talking to themselves as they thrilled to the film. If he handed out, say, a dozen guns to likely-looking subjects (and his Intelligence experience made Strode a very shrewd judge of men) there was a good chance that six of them at least would not be able to resist firing the bloody things off. He had seen the film in the West End, and knew how exactly it suited his purpose. It was actually about a gang of pot-shot killers – tailor-made to enable him to turn Whitgate into a centre of mindless slaying and maiming.

That, then, had been Strode's plan – and up until this

moment, everything had gone according to it, as unerringly as his bullet had travelled to the dead centre of Fordyce's forehead.

But pot-shooters didn't aim unerringly.

And they very seldom fired just once.

So Strode raised his revolver again, and emptied the remaining five chambers on the street below. By the time he had finished, Sir Gilbert's sprawling body had company. A constable was lying across it, shot in the groin; a girl in the Jeremy Caxton entourage was reeling back by the entrance doors, blood pouring from her thigh; two panes of glass in the Civic Centre windows had been smashed, and the plaster bust of some civic worthy, above the entrance, had been given a bullet in the eye.

Just mindless pot-shooting by a trigger-happy yobbo – that was what Strode intended it to look like. But, skilled psychologist though he was, he had left one thing out of his calculations: the fact that a lot of people on the steps, in both political camps, were at heart trigger-happy yobbos themselves.

Before Strode's last shot had rung out, guns had appeared in more than half a dozen hands – and two or three policemen had drawn revolvers too.

A hail of bullets cracked into the sign on the Underground roof – some of them fired from a sense of duty, some in hatred, some in panic, some in sheer hysteria.

None of them hit Strode, who was already at the rear of the roof, executing his carefully-planned leap down into the blind alley. But one of them, aimed ten feet too low, hit an Underground ticket-collector in the shoulder. Another ricocheted and wounded a newsvendor on the right of the station entrance. Yet another was so wildly off-target that it slammed through Lemaitre's window across the street.

Not that Lemaitre was any longer there. He was down-stairs, rushing out of the police station entrance with Inspector Skelton, the uniformed officer in charge of the station. About a dozen uniformed men were behind them. Skelton, a sour-faced, normally taciturn man in his late forties, had had a vast experience of Whitgate and its riots, and gave the impression that nothing could surprise or shake him. But he was looking shaken now, and for once was almost talkative.

"Godalmighty, Lem," he murmured, so softly that the words came out more like a prayer than an oath. "Talk about law and order breaking down . . . "

Lemaitre needed no telling what he meant. There they were, right outside a police station, looking across at a Civic Centre whose steps were lined with more policemen. Yet the police were being totally ignored by the fanatics of both the Left and the Right.

Jeremy Caxton had turned back from the entrance and was at the top of the steps, where his supporters had formed a protective ring round him. Sir Gilbert Fordyce's followers, leaving the body of their dead leader lying across the lower steps like a figure from an old Italian painting, were marching menacingly upon the Caxtonites, fists clenched, the occasional gun gleaming in the sun. Perhaps they believed that Caxton had ordered Fordyce's assassination. Perhaps it was a simple gut reaction - their leader was dead, why should their enemy's leader continue to live? Whatever the reason, there was no mistaking the depth of their hatred, the implacable intensity of their purpose. Two policemen kneeling by the wounded constable, and another tending the wounded girl, were in danger of being trampled on . . .

Lemaitre was suddenly, agonisingly aware that he and

Skelton had only seconds in which to bring the situation under control, or else –

Two shots completed the thought for him, and three more rang out before he and Skelton were halfway across the street.

But then, suddenly, there was a surprise interruption. A stentorian voice barked:

"Stop it, you bloody fools! STOP!"

And Fordyce's followers *did* stop – at least for a moment.

Some of them turned right round in their tracks – to stare at a tall, military figure who had come striding out of some alley, and was now standing in the road only about ten yards to Lemaitre's right, glaring at them with a fury that mirrored their own.

"Who the hell's that?" Lemaitre breathed.

Skelton's sour features actually broke into a smile of relief, and he became more talkative than ever.

"He's Fordyce's deputy," he told Lemaitre. "Much more moderate man than Sir Gilbert. There were often bitter quarrels between them, I believe . . . I suppose he's the BGBM's leader now – if you ask me, it's a good job too."

Carried away by his enthusiasm, Skelton actually gripped Lemaitre's arm.

"Look at the way he's stopped those Fascist thugs – with just one shout! Believe me, if there's anyone who can save us from a bloodbath here in Whitgate, it's Major Robert Strode . . . "

11 "Who Are You?"

"No," said Gideon, very firmly.

Acutely aware of the despair his answer was causing in the minds of all three of his hearers - Alec and Penny, as well as Matt, who had made the suggestion - he tried hard to soften the blow.

"I know you think I'm opposed to new techniques on principle. As it happens, I'm not. I have always welcomed any new ideas that really promised to get results. And in this situation, we need results so desperately that I'm just about ready to try anything . . . " His voice suddenly gruff, he added: "Anything but that."

There was a long, painful pause, broken by a little sob from Penny. For a moment, Gideon thought she was going to get up and dash out of the room, and he wouldn't have blamed her. Poor girl, she had had as nerve-wracking a day as it was possible for a mother to experience. Rushed home from the recording studios in a police car, she had been almost immediately confronted by B.B.C. and I.T.V. news cameras, and had had to fight back her hysteria and broadcast a personal appeal to the kidnappers. The rest of the day she had spent walking up and down, round and round the house, waiting desperately for a ransom call that never came. Hundreds of other calls had come, though – from people who believed they had spotted the baby or the black Ford Capri; from worried wellwishers by the dozen, and from cranks and hoaxers by the dozen, too. Penny had played her full part in coping with them. She had also spent some time by her mother's bedside, too . . . watching Kate as even in her drugged sleep, she tossed and turned . . .

"Dad," she suddenly burst out. "I'm as worried about Mum as you are . . . and the last thing I want to do is place her in any danger . . . but couldn t you at least ring the doctor and get his advice instead of turning down Matt's suggestion out of hand?"

"I'll ring him if you like," said Gideon. "But it's obvious what'll he say. He's told me that Kate must be kept away from all stress and strain. To bring her downstairs as soon as she wakes up – and confront her with – " Gideon nearly choked " – a ruddy *hypnotist,* for God's sake . . . I'm sorry, but all of you must see that the only possible answer is the one I've given. *No.*"

"Do you think," said Alec softly, "that that's the answer Kate herself would give if we were to wake her up and ask her?"

Gideon made no reply. He seemed hardly to hear the question, but just sat staring down at the table in front of him.

They were in Alec's study, which had been converted into a

110

temporary police headquarters, sitting round a boardroom-like table, on which stood a battery of extra telephones, installed that day by Post Office engineers.

Two of the phones connected directly with Scotland Yard, and Gideon and Alec had used them frequently throughout the day, Alec for long conversations with Scott-Marle, Gideon for equally long talks with Paul Barnaby, who had kept him abreast of developments everywhere, including Whitgate, where the news had seemed to be good. The facts about the current developments there had not yet percolated through. Two other phones had been kept busy with the flood of incoming calls, which Alec had dealt with personally, except when the caller particularly wanted to speak to Penny. Anonymous calls claiming to be from the kidnappers were switched to the living room, and fed through the complex network of computer equipment. (There had been six of these calls, but all the speakers had rapidly betrayed themselves as hoaxers.) Calls from people claiming to have seen the baby, or to have spotted the car, were taped and sent down to Fulham police station. It was there that an increasingly distraught Matt Honiwell had spent most of the day, sending out C.I.D. men to check up on anything that looked remotely like a valid lead.

Matt had also spent some hours in the records department of Scotland Yard, attempting to build up a list of criminals known to be harbouring a grudge against Hobbs or Gideon. But since between them the two had virtually directed the whole of the C.I.D.'s war against crime for upwards of ten years, the list rapidly grew so large that the operation became almost pointless.

In fact, as the day wore on and hope after hope had shrivelled like the last of the lilac blossoms under the scorching

111

sun, one thing had become clearer and clearer to Matt.

Their only hope of making any progress whatsoever in this case was somehow to get at the facts locked up in Kate Gideon's brain. She had had a good long look straight down at the kidnapper's car. Her conscious mind had registered the fact that it was a black Ford Capri. But there was a chance that her subconscious mind had registered a good deal more, perhaps even the number of the car. Then there was the question of the shadowy figure in the back of the Capri – a figure whom she *thought* she had recognised . . .

Matt had never forgotten a kidnapping case which had been finally solved with the help of an E.S.P. man called Jacob Brodnik. Somehow Brodnik's brain had received an image sent out by the subconscious mind of a kidnapped girl, even though she was heavily drugged and near to death at the time.* A seemingly hopeless case had been transformed by unorthodox help. Perhaps it was time to call in that sort of help again. While he had been at the Yard, he had made inquiries about hypnosis. He discovered that it was used by the Met in more than ninety cases a year. And in at least half these cases, witnesses had remembered under trance conditions vital facts which had evaded their conscious minds.

He had been given the name of a good hypnotist – an ex-Harley Street doctor named Rodney Bennett. He had rung Bennett, and found that he was free. He had even asked about the possible danger of hypnosis to a heart patient.

"Danger?" Bennett had replied. "Why should there be danger? Hypnosis relaxes and relieves tension. It does not normally add to strain . . . "

Armed with these facts, Matt had approached Alec and

*Gideon's Force

Penny, who had both jumped at the idea of hypnotism being used.

"I warn you," Penny had said. "You won't find Dad so easy to persuade."

"But perhaps," Alec had added, "if we got George into my study, and made a concerted effort - all three of us . . . "

Well, they had made their concerted effort, Matt told himself wearily, and it had failed. As he knew from long experience, when George said "no", he meant "no", and nothing short of a miracle was likely to change his mind.

The silence dragged on and on.

Finally Alec could bear it no longer, and rather sharply repeated his question.

"I asked you, George, what answer you thought *Kate* would give."

Gideon at last looked up.

"She'd say 'yes' like a shot," he admitted. "And if I was *sure* her heart would stand it, so would I."

Matt had one last try.

"But I told you, George, what Rodney Bennett said about hypnosis easing strain."

Gideon was suddenly standing.

"I'm sorry, but neither Bennett nor anyone else can convince me that reliving a moment of terror is going to ease anyone's strain. I just *can't* let Kate - "

He broke off. A strange sound filled the room, a sound that made Gideon's heart turn over, and Penny's face lose even the faint traces of colour that remained in it.

They had left the door open, so that they could hear at once if Kate woke up and called out. The spare bedroom where she was lying was immediately above the study.

She was calling out now all right - but it sounded as if she

113

was doing it in her sleep, from the depths of some indescribable nightmare.

"Who are you?" she was screaming. "*Who - are - you?*"

Gideon led the headlong rush upstairs, and reached the bedroom seconds ahead of the others.

Kate had been tossing and turning with such ferocity that the coverlet which Miss Thompson had wrapped round her was now on the floor, on the far side of the room. Kate was half sitting up now, her eyes wide open, staring at something – or someone – which only she could see.

As Gideon put an arm round her, she started violently and woke up. (It was more than seven hours since she had been given the sedative injection, Gideon remembered. It should be wearing off by now.)

"Oh, it's you, love," she said, dazedly. "I thought it was the man in the black Capri. I kept trying to see his face, but there was nothing there – just a great white blank. Lord, what a nightmare. I suppose the dream was trying to make me remember who he was . . . Oh, George, if only I *could* remember . . . "

Gideon sat down beside her, took her hand, and stroked it gently, reassuringly. He knew now that there was only one possible decision that he could take. Nothing could be more dangerous for Kate than to go on like this.

"With luck, you *will* be remembering – very soon," he said, and turned to Matt, who was just visible behind Alec and Penny in the doorway. "Get on to that Rodney Bennett and get him here. Straight away."

114

12 Gun Game

"Stop it, you bloody fools . . ."

Those words, shouted in Strode's parade-ground bellow, had paralysed all the BGBM followers – except one: a thick-necked, shaven-headed youth of about eighteen, wearing a black motorcycling outfit covered with heavy metal studs. Seconds before, when that first fatal shot had run out, this youth had been at Fordyce's side, and his leader had almost literally fallen at his feet. Probably he had been Sir Gilbert's personal bodyguard, and obviously he had hero-worshipped him. His face, with its thick lips, low forehead and jutting jaw, seemed built to look vicious and aggressive; but there were tears in his eyes as well as hate, and his voice trembled with grief, even though the words spat contempt. It was a grotesque combination of emotions, and a frightening one, thought Lemaitre. A boy torn apart like that could easily become dangerously hysterical – and in this sort of situation, hysteria could spread like a forest fire.

Stepping down from the steps on to the road and facing
Strode, almost as if the two of them were poised to fight a
duel, the youth yelled, "Just who are you calling a bloody
fool?"

Angrily, Strode barked back, "The whole lot of you,
Johnson, the whole stupid lot of you!"

Walking up and down in front of them like an officer
addressing a parade, he started to harangue the whole BGBM
mob.

"Haven't you heard about the pot-shot maniacs who are
plaguing this town? Surely it's obvious that the killer on the
roof was one of that pathetic, mindless brigade."

"*Is* it, Major?"

The youth Strode had called "Johnson" walked a few yards
back up the steps. He had now returned to the spot where the
body of his leader lay sprawling. (The injured constable who
had originally fallen across Fordyce had been carried away.)

Very dramatically, as an odd silence fell over the whole
street, Johnson pointed to the bullet wound in Fordyce's
forehead. Just for a moment, his grief gave him a weird, tragic
dignity. He might have been Mark Antony pointing to the
stab wounds of the fallen Caesar.

What he said was hardly a Mark Antony oration, but it was
effective, nonetheless. In a thick, sneering voice, he shouted,
"F . . . . . g good aiming that, for a pot-shooter, don't you
reckon, Major? Makes me think it was someone just *pretending*
to be a pot-shooter . . . "

For a moment, Strode was so taken aback that he could
hardly speak. It was almost as though Johnson was on the
brink of accusing *him*. His only course was to change all his
plans – and, at whatever the cost, to direct suspicion
elsewhere.

116

He joined Johnson beside Fordyce's body, stared down at it for a moment, and then told the crowd, "This boy is right. This is no pot-shot killing. It's a cold-blooded assassination – and do any of you have to be told who ordered it?"

With a dramatically shaking hand, he pointed up the steps, to where Jeremy Caxton was still standing, surrounded by a circle of protecting followers.

At the top of his stentorian voice, Strode bellowed, "*That murdering Commie bastard there!*"

An angry roar went up from the BGBM supporters. It sounded halfway between a *Sieg Heil* and the howl of a pack of famished wolves.

But a counter-roar came from the Caxton supporters at the top of the steps. Caxton himself, red in the face and waving his incongruous cigar, yelled: "Forward with the people! Death to all Fascist pigs!"

It was almost as though he was proudly claiming responsibility for the killing. His followers picked up the slogan, and shouting "Forward with the people!" actually moved forward down the steps, until the BGBM men, now in an almost murderous frenzy, started to drive them back.

The uniformed police, who had been lining the steps, were simply thrust aside. But Inspector Skelton, who was equipped with a walkie-talkie, began barking orders. The policemen rallied, and started to wade in, their helmets sticking up above the milling crowd like breakwater posts rising out of a churning sea.

Suddenly Strode had a revolver in his hand.

"Get him! Get the murdering Commie!" he yelled, and with the near-hysterical Johnson beside him, was about to rush up the steps and plunge into the battle, when Lemaitre calmly stepped forward and put a hand on his arm.

117

"I'm a police officer and I'll take that weapon, if you don't mind," he said levelly. "And I'm afraid I must ask you to accompany me to the police station."

Lemaitre had, as usual, acted on impulse - and, as usual, was almost instantly regretting it.

Although there were now more than sixty constables struggling with the mobs further up the steps, and although the police station itself was only about twenty yards away across the street, he was himself quite alone and in a very vulnerable position. Skelton had disappeared into the crowd; so had the dozen constables who had been behind him. All Lemaitre could see, on all sides, were leather-jacketed youths of the Johnson type, with Johnson himself leading them. Swiftly and silently they formed themselves into a circle around him and Strode; a circle that was steadily closing in.

It was Strode, though, not Lemaitre, who was starting to sweat with fear. He was realising what a crazy, reckless move it had been to bring out that gun. If it got into the hands of the police, and the ballistic experts checked it with the bullet that had killed Fordyce . . .

He hoped desperately that his sweat didn't show. If ever there was a time to play it cool, it was now.

"Should I let the gentleman have my gun, boys?" he asked playfully. "It's not much use to me - there are no bullets in it." To prove his point, he pressed the trigger; there was only an echoing click, as he had known there would be, because he had emptied the gun when firing from the roof. "Or shall we make him jump about for it?" he went on, mockingly. "Here, somebody - catch!"

Before Lemaitre could stop him, he had tossed the revolver to the nearest skinhead, and the next moment, it was being passed round and round the circle, to the accompaniment of jeering and, in one or two cases, actual spitting.

Lemaitre made a couple of attempts to grab the gun, but he wasn't as fast as he had been in his young days, and it eluded him. In the process, he turned his back for a moment on the Major, who made very full use of that moment indeed.

He pressed a key into the palm of Johnson's right hand, whispering: "You know what to do?"

Johnson said nothing. He just nodded and pocketed the key which, as he was well aware, would unlock the door of the BGBM secret armoury, and enable him to make a massive distribution of guns. For the first time Johnson began to respect his new leader. He had always thought Strode a lily-livered weakling, lacking Sir Gilbert Fordyce's iron will and eagerness for war. Now it seemed that he was ready to make the streets of Whitgate run with blood to avenge the murdered Fordyce. Johnson's eyes gleamed with excitement – and something more. It was almost as if he was transferring his hero-worship from the dead to the living, from Fordyce to the Iron Major.

Strode noticed the look of dumb, adoring allegiance – as unexpected as tears on that vicious skinhead face – and responded with a faint smile. As leader of the BGBM, the last thing he wanted was a shoot-out with the WUW. He had created the whole pot-shot terror expressly to avoid it. But things were different now. He had himself been forced to announce publicly that the bullet that had killed Fordyce couldn't have been a pot-shot. It wouldn't be long before awkward facts began to emerge – the fact that he was known to be an expert marksman, that he had had a long and bitter feud with Fordyce, and that he had been strangely absent from the scene when the shooting had occurred. His only hope was to build himself up at Fordyce's implacable avenger, to let all issues become confused amidst the smoke and blood of war . . .

That gun, for instance, still being passed around the circle . . . At the moment it was as dangerous to him as if it were fully loaded, and pointed directly at his head. But if it wound up in the pocket of some skinhead BGBM follower and became just one of the fifty or more guns being used in a mass shoot-out tonight, then how could it ever be traced back to him?

The luck was with him, Strode noticed. One of the gang of skinheads *had* pocketed the revolver. The gun game was over. Another game was beginning, and a still more sinister one, from this police officer's point of view. The circle was closing in on him menacingly. One or two flick-knives flashed . . .

Lemaitre stared at them contemptuously. He was strongly tempted to start a scrap, but he would be heavily outnumbered, and doubted if he could duck and swerve as smartly as he used to do in his East End youth. He decided to try to impress them instead – a rare thing for him to try, but there was a time and place for everything.

"I should warn you all that I am Chief Detective Superintendent Lemaitre, in charge of the whole North London police division," he said grimly. "That means, if you need to have it spelt out, that if anything happens to me, quite a lot will subsequently happen to each and every one of you. Have I made myself clear?"

Apparently he had. The circle abruptly stopped closing in, and even widened a little.

The Major, smiling blandly now, lived up to the reputation Skelton had given him for being a moderate, an anti-bloodbath man.

"Put those away, boys," he said to the skinheads with the

flick-knives, "and I'm sure Mr. Lemaitre will pretend he hasn't seen them." Turning back to Lemaitre, he added smoothly, with the bland smile growing, "I've some good news for you, my friend. I've decided, in that time-honoured phrase, to come quietly." Very much less smoothly, he added, "As long as you assure me that you will be taking in that murderer, Jeremy Caxton, too." (He dared not allow himself to be the only one arrested. Tongues might wag. The rumour might start that he was himself suspected of the Fordyce murder . . .)

Almost anyone else in the Metropolitan Police Force – Gideon included – would have thought long and hard about having the two most dangerous rabble-rousers in London in one police station at the same time, with their respective mobs already tangling in the street outside.

But Lemaitre, being Lemaitre, didn't think at all.

"Don't you worry, Strode. We'll bring him in – and everyone else responsible for this outrageous breach of the peace," he said.

The circle broke, and a few seconds later, he was conducting a smiling Strode in through the door of the police station.

Twenty minutes later, he and Skelton, with half a dozen constables lending a hand, were dragging a shouting and screaming Caxton through the same door.

By that time, in police jargon, "order had been restored" to Whitgate High Street. The force of nearly a hundred uniformed men, most of whom (at Gideon's suggestion) had been armed, had proved just big enough to get the better of the mobs. Dozens of names had been taken, but few arrests made; Lemaitre had gone for the leaders, not the rabble. The angry mobs themselves had vanished, leaving only a few desultory groups standing around, staring at nothing in particular through the deepening dusk. The wounded had been rushed to hospital, the body of Sir Gilbert to a mortuary. Police photographers with flash equipment were working on the steps where Fordyce had fallen, the whole area had been cordoned off, and chalkmarks drawn where the body had sprawled. C.I.D. men were swarming into the Underground station, and forensic experts – fingerprint men and others – were already busy round the circular sign on the roof, working under hastily rigged electric bulbs. Derek Price was in charge of this operation; Lemaitre was using him for everything important that he couldn't superintend himself, and was keeping him so busy that for the first time in thirteen weeks anxious thoughts about Anne Swanleigh and her father had almost faded from his mind. It surely couldn't be long before he was off duty and on his way to see them, in any case . . .

The Underground sign itself had not been switched on, to save Price's team from dazzle. This was annoying the small army of TV cameramen who had now arrived in the street below, and were trying to film the spot where all the trouble had begun.

There did not seem to be any trouble around now. But *two* people walking away from the street had keys in their pockets: *both* mobs would return around midnight with almost every member armed with a loaded gun.

No one outside the BGBM and the WUW knew this for certain, but there were some other members of the public who could sense the pent-up hatred in the air, who could read the telltale signs that this dusk was darkening into what could be the blackest night in London history.

For example, leaning in a doorway about a hundred yards along the High Street, a youth with an odd, white, mask-like face was preparing himself for a long wait, in the hope that there would be some kind of action at the end.

He was preparing himself for that action now – by chalking on the wall beside him: "SHOOT TO KILL".

*   *   *

Two miles away, in a short stretch of backstreet in Pimlico, there was an even more sinister calm.

Although it was now deep dusk, no lights had been turned on in the Swanleigh shop or in the house behind it.

And because the stake-out was empty and the street deserted, there had been no one to hear the strange sounds that had come from the shop just before its 8.0 p.m. closing time – and after which both house and shop had been as silent as the grave.

The sounds of a scream, a scuffle, a faint low moan of anguish . . . and a softly bouncing ball.

13 Hypnosis

Not many in London were facing the night ahead with more
anxiety than Gideon. Indeed, the hour ahead was fraught with
so many nightmarish possibilities that the only way to keep
going was to shut his mind to them.

He had never been hypnotised, or seen anyone hypnotised,
or even met a hypnotist in his life. There was therefore no
personal experience whatever that he could draw on to tell
him what he was letting Kate in for; what risks he was
allowing her to run. Common sense told him, though, that
there had to be great risk in a woman with a weak heart
reliving the moment that had caused her to collapse. Was he
right in gambling that the strain of not remembering that face
constituted an even greater risk to Kate?

One thing, at least, suggested that he might have gambled
right. Kate herself was delighted at the idea of being
hypnotised. Momentarily, at least, all trace of anxiety had
gone from her face. Those grey-blue eyes of hers had
recaptured a little of the calmness and serenity which had

always been their special quality. It wasn't, of course, that she had forgotten about the baby George. It was just that at last something positive was being done to advance the inquiry – and by undergoing the hypnosis she, Kate, was the one who was doing it!

There was no possibility of keeping her in bed for a moment longer. She was up and about, bustling around the house and discussing the arrangements for the hypnotist's visit almost as if she was planning a social occasion. With the living room full of sound equipment, and Alec's study being used as a police H.Q., the only room in the house suitable for the consultation, she decided, was the dining room.

"Do you think one can be hypnotised in a dining room chair?" she asked. "Or does one have to lie on a couch? In that case, perhaps two chairs could be put together . . . "

Penny actually laughed – for the first time since she had arrived back home in that police car.

"Don't be so silly, Mum. Of course you'll have to have a couch. In fact, I think Alec could clear a corner of the living room. There – " Her voice faltered slightly, and suddenly she wasn't laughing any more. "There obviously isn't going to be a call from the kidnappers after all."

Alec nodded.

"The living room would be ideal," he said. "We've already good video equipment in there, and can tape the whole session."

This was too much for Gideon.

"Over my body, you'll tape it!" he suddenly roared. "Under hypnosis, all sorts of private thoughts come out. Kate won't want them on public display. Can't you understand that – or is privacy something that's not allowed in your brave new videotape world?"

He was surprised at - and rather ashamed of - the fury in his voice. This was no time to launch a bitter argument about Hobbs's new techniques, no matter how much he resented them.

"Calm down, love," said Kate, her own eyes now calmer than ever. "I don't mind being videotaped in the least. I shall feel like a film star."

"Apart from that, George, it makes *sense*," said Alec. "Penny and Matt and I can't all be in the room during the session. Kate *would* feel she was giving a public performance then! On the other hand, she might mutter something indistinctly that contains a vital clue - and if all of us could hear and see her doing it, one of us might be able to decipher it. And there'll be no embarrassment, George. No one will be working the camera. It'll just be focused on the couch and left running, like a tape recorder. That's the technique we use in the interrogation rooms, of course . . . "

There was no denying the force of these arguments, and Gideon gave way; although when he watched the living room being prepared - the couch being put in position, a lamp stand being brought up to shine directly down on it, and the video camera being wheeled in front of it - he could not help his sense of dread returning. It was though he had strayed into some science fiction nightmare, in which Kate - *his* Kate - was going to be snatched away from him and put at the mercy of unknown, alien forces.

But if she hadn't been so willing to go through with it, for the sake of the baby, then she wouldn't have *been* Kate, he supposed. Times changed, ideas changed, methods changed - but some things never altered, or, at least, were endlessly renewed, and Kate's calm courage was one of them. It was time he let a little of it rub off on him, he told himself - and stepping forward, helped Penny to adjust the cushions on the couch.

While he was doing this, Alec was called to the phone. He returned, grim-faced, with a report of the assassination of Fordyce and the riot in Whitgate High Street.

"The assassin got away, and no one even glimpsed his face. Lem thinks it was one of the pot-shot maniacs, but the crowd didn't believe that, and I can't say I blame them. Fordyce died from a bullet drilled through the middle of his forehead, which sounds like skilled marksmanship to me."

"And to me," Gideon said.

An idea was beginning to form at the back of his mind. Perhaps the whole pot-shot business had been started deliberately as a *cover* for the assassination . . .

But he had no time to develop the idea. Alec was rushing on.

"Good job we'd taken your advice and had a hundred armed men from Uniform there. They restored order in under a quarter of an hour. Lem has taken both Jeremy Caxton and the new Back to Great Britain leader, a Major Robert Strode, to the police station for questioning. And everything's very quiet in Whitgate High Street now."

Gideon raised an eyebrow.

"You mean there are no protesters outside the police station at all? Nobody so much as going *Sieg Heil* or giving a Commie raised-fist gesture?"

"I don't think so," said Alec. "Probably they realised that the police would move them along pretty sharpish if they did."

Gideon frowned.

"One leader gets shot, two more get arrested – and the two most violent political mobs in Britain just riot for a quarter of an hour, and then shrug their shoulders and go home? I don't believe it, Alec - and I don't like it. Lem's sitting on a load of dynamite - and I think someone ought to tell him so. Not that it's easy to tell Lem anything . . . until it's too late - ''

He broke off. He suddenly had the feeling that he was sitting on a load of dynamite himself.

Matt was leading a tall, white-haired, rather fatherly man into the room, and taking him straight across to Kate.

"Mrs. Gideon, this is Dr. Rodney Bennett," he said.

*   *   *

Dr. Bennett certainly knew his job.

Despite the extreme tension in the air, not helped by the presence of the video camera, it took him less than two minutes to establish a relaxed, consulting-room atmosphere.

"No, there's no need to lie down if you don't want to, Mrs. Gideon. The psychiatrist's couch went out with the Victorian *chaise longue*, and in any case, I'm no psychiatrist! My business is not to heal minds, but to set them free . . . Your deeper self, your true self is, as it were, bound and gagged by all your conscious worries and frustrations. My task is to unfasten the ropes, strip off the gag, and let it speak."

"I only hope," murmured Kate, "that you'll find it's got something to say."

Moving with her special grace, she seated herself at one end of the couch. Penny, Alec and Matt crept out of the room, leaving Gideon as the only audience - if one forgot the video camera. Since it was totally soundless in operation, it was, in fact, becoming easier and easier to forget that it was there at all.

"Our deeper selves always have something to say, Mrs. Gideon," Bennett continued. "They are much closer observers than our conscious minds. They see much more, they remember much more, I sometimes think they *know* much more."

Gideon noticed that Bennett was talking in a curious, rhythmic way, almost as though he was reciting poetry. He noticed something even more curious: Kate was nodding her head to and fro in time to his words. Her eyes were half closed. She looked rather as if she had had a glass of wine too many, and was feeling half drowsy, half tipsy.

She began to repeat Bennett's words.

"I – I must try to remember that, Doctor. They see much more . . . they remember much more . . . they . . . know . . . "

Her words faded, and for a moment, Gideon thought she had gone to sleep. But her eyes were wide open, and she was staring straight in front of her, quite obviously in a trance. Bennett confirmed her state by waving a hand six inches in front of her eyes. She did not so much as blink.

"Your wife is a very good subject, Commander," he said gently. "Sensitive people usually are – especially if they are under a lot of strain. In such circumstances, the hard-pressed conscious mind doesn't need much persuading to lay down its burden and hand over to its hidden partner."

"H'm. I suppose not," said Gideon gruffly.

He could not pretend that he liked any part of this. At what seemed to be the merest flick of this man's finger, Kate had been turned into a silent, staring zombie – someone he couldn't talk to, couldn't reach; someone who would not even feel it if he squeezed her hand. It was one of the most unnerving moments he had ever experienced. The only thing that made it bearable was the fact that a faint smile played

129

around Kate's mouth, and that she looked more relaxed than at any time since the kidnapping - far more relaxed, even, than during that sedated sleep.

Bennett had taken a small notebook from his pocket, and now he started to consult it.

"Let me see . . . what time do you want Mrs. Gideon to regress to?"

"What time - ?"

It took Gideon a moment to interpret the doctor's jargon, and longer to bring himself to reply. At length, "The kidnapping occurred between twelve noon and twelve-thirty today," he said. "If - if you could take her mind back to then, I think that should tell us all we need to know."

"Right," Bennett said. "I think it would be best to go back beyond that, right to the beginning of the day, and then move forward gradually to the disturbing part . . . "

He turned to Kate, his voice still soft and reassuring, but now with an unmistakable hint of command behind it.

"Can you hear me, Mrs. Gideon?"

"Yes. Yes, I can hear you."

"Then you and I are going to play a little game."

"A little game, yes."

Kate sounded pathetically eager, like a child.

"We're going to pretend that it is no longer night time, but first thing this morning."

"First thing this morning, yes."

"Now I want you to tell me where you are and what you're doing."

"I'm in bed, waking up," Kate said. "There's - bright sunlight shining through the curtains . . . dazzling . . . " She made a face, and clapped both hands to her ears. "Oh, that

130

whistling kettle - it's ear-splitting. George must have left it on and forgotten about it. I'd better get downstairs before it boils dry."

"You're going downstairs now?"

"Yes . . . yes - and now I'm in the kitchen, making tea . . . and . . . and now I'm drinking it, with - "

Suddenly Kate sat upright, and seemed to be talking, not to Bennett, but to some invisible person in front of her.

"I've never known a back seat you didn't bulge out of, love," she said laughing. "And I don't think anyone - least of all Alec - would have it any other way."

Gideon felt so many icy tingles in his scalp that he wasn't sure his hair wasn't actually standing on end. Kate could not see him, sitting here beside her; but she could see, and talk to, an image of him as he had been at half past seven that morning! It was almost like being, literally, in two places at once, an experience so unnerving that it was all he could do to stop himself calling off the experiment there and then.

Kate's mind seemed to be jumping forward in time now. She raised a hand, as if holding an invisible telephone to her ear, and began repeating, word for word, what she'd said when she'd rung him up at the Yard that morning.

"It's so hot that I'm almost tempted to borrow one of Penny's swimsuits and start sunbathing. Or do you think that sort of thing's ridiculous at my age?"

There was a pause, and she burst out laughing. Obviously, thought Gideon, she had just heard again that remark of his about giving the neighbours too much of a treat.

There was another pause, a very tense one. Kate's mood changed dramatically. Suddenly she was closer to sobbing than laughing, and her hands were trembling. She had obviously reached the moment when she'd run upstairs to find a swim-

131

suit, and then had looked out of the window, and –

"Quick!" said Gideon to Bennett. "Ask her what she can see."

The doctor turned to Kate.

"Tell me where you are now."

"In Penny's bedroom, by the window. There's a car – a car by the garden gate."

"What kind of car, Mrs. Gideon?"

"A large black Ford Capri."

"Can you see its number?"

"Number? Oh, yes. VNP 244P."

Gideon's heart leapt. This was the first proof positive that hypnotism worked: that the subconscious mind *could* retain more memories than the conscious one . . .

Kate was getting very agitated now. Her whole body was trembling, shaking the couch.

"There's something funny going on. The left-hand back door is open, and the driver's keeping the engine running. It's as if they are crooks of some sort . . . bank robbers or – oh, my God – *kidnappers* . . . "

Kate's face was turning very pale. There was a terrifying blueness round her lips. This couldn't go on, thought Gideon. He didn't *dare* let it go on.

"We must stop this," he whispered to the doctor. "*Now*."

Bennett nodded, and turned once more to Kate.

"Can you hear me, Mrs. Gideon. When I've counted to five, I want you to wake up . . . "

But it seemed as if Kate couldn't hear him. She was too deeply lost in that agonising moment from the past, couldn't tear herself away from that remembered window, couldn't stop staring down in fascinated horror at the car.

"There's someone in the back, keeping well away from the windows . . ."

Bennett stood up, his gentle voice suddenly deep and authoritative.

"I'm starting to count now, Mrs. Gideon. At five you wake up, remember? *One* . . ."

"Wait. I seem to – to know his face . . . He's – he's – "

"*Two . . . Three . . . Four . . .*"

Beads of sweat broke out on Gideon's forehead, turning instantly into what felt like droplets of ice. He raised his hand to signal Bennett to stop the countdown, or at least slow it down, but then he looked at Kate's face, and the hand dropped to his side. He couldn't let her run these risks, not for a second longer, even if that second *was* vital to the case.

"*Five*," said Bennett – and instantly, Kate was wide awake.

Now that it was over, she seemed little the worse for her experience. The blueness was fading from her lips, the colour coming back into her cheeks. Her eyes were rather dazed, but calm and not distraught; they suggested that the nightmare and near-hysteria were back where they belonged – in the past.

One thing, though, had remained with her from the last moments of her trance: a name which, for some reason, she could not help repeating.

"*Farrant. John Farrant. John Farrant,*" Kate found herself saying, over and over again.

14　Farrant

John Farrant.

It was months since Gideon had last heard that name; he had hoped never to hear it again.

Less than a year before, Farrant had been one of the most successful Chief Detective Superintendents in the C.I.D. Still in his middle thirties, with crinkly black hair and sharp grey eyes, he had also been one of the best-looking men in the department, even though his features were so sharp that his face had often reminded Gideon of the old joke about two profiles stuck together. His relentless drive and ambition – coupled with an intense and obvious eagerness to please – had impressed so many high-ups that his rise at the Yard had been meteoric.

But somehow, he had always failed to impress Gideon, who only admired ambition when it was accompanied by humanity, a quality which, he had sensed, Farrant conspicuously lacked.

Soon enough, events had proved him right. Evidence had piled up, suggesting (though not proving) that Farrant had been guilty of brutally beating up a suspect during interrogation. Finally Gideon had caught him red-handed faking a piece of evidence.*

Farrant had still tried to justify himself. There had been no other way, he said, to make sure the charges stuck on a badly wanted man.

Gideon still remembered his own withering reply.

"No. There never is any other way for you, Farrant, is there, except the lying way, the cheating way, the bullying way. Your sort bring contempt on the C.I.D. So don't blame me if just for once I bring some down on you. You are suspended from this minute . . . "

He had turned on his heel and walked away – but not before he had caught the look on Farrant's face. It was a look so curious that the memory of it had stayed with him ever since.

None of the expected emotions – shock, shame, anger, hatred, resentment, fury – had been there. Farrant seemed to have withdrawn into himself, like a tortoise into a shell, but his narrowed eyes suggested that he was thinking furiously.

It was as if, right in that first second of defeat, he was already starting to calculate how he could overcome this setback to his career; how he could resume his climb to the top.

And perhaps – how he could get his revenge.

*   *   *

When Dr. Bennett had been seen out, by a very grateful Gideon, Matt Honiwell called an immediate council of war

* *Gideon's Law*

in Alec's study. Kate and Penny were present as well as the men.

"I gather from your expression, George," said Matt, "that Kate has named the man in the Ford Capri."

"She has," said Gideon. "And it's a name we know only too well. Tell 'em, love."

Kate repeated the name once again – but not dazedly this time. She had been thinking about it hard.

"He was that bent detective you got suspended last year, wasn't he? No wonder I had such a job remembering the face. I believe I've only seen him once – and that was at a C.I.D. dinner where you introduced me to all the staff."

Penny nodded.

"I was there with Alec, so I probably saw him too. But I don't think I'd have remembered him in your place – even under hypnosis." She was suddenly nearly crying. "But – but why should this man have done this terrible thing? He was very ambitious, I've always heard. Well – this isn't going to get him his job back, is it – or help him in any way? What do you think's happened? That his resentment at Dad for suspending him has just sent him round the bend?"

Gideon, Matt and Alec glanced at each other. Each of them had his own memories of Farrant, and each was recalling moments when his extraordinary restlessness and eagerness to please had made them wonder if there was something pathologically wrong with his mental make-up. There were other troubling facts they all remembered, too: stories of Farrant's callousness and brutality. It wasn't only suspects under interrogation who had suffered at his hands. His wife, a pretty, fragile-looking blonde called Jill, had often been seen with strange bruises, which she had explained away rather lamely by saying she was accident prone about the home . . .

136

Penny was not slow to notice these glances.

"That's what you all think, isn't it? That he *is* a psychopath - "

Matt hurriedly interrupted her. With his most reassuring smile - and no one at the Yard, thought Gideon, could smile more reassuringly than Matt - he said gently, "It's a possibility we've got to consider, but there are many others. You could well have been right with your first guess - that the kidnapping is part of some devious, carefully calculated plot to further Farrant's ambition."

"Certainly," Hobbs agreed, "that's the theory that fits in most closely with the John Farrant *I* knew. The man was a positively fanatical careerist. You could almost say that his driving ambition drove everything else out of his life. But suspension, which led to him being compelled to resign, must have been very like a death blow to him."

"No, it wasn't," Gideon said softly. "Curiously enough, he hardly seemed to feel it. Almost before I'd finished telling him what was going to happen to him, I could see that he was miles away, busily planning his next move." He started. "Incidentally, what *was* his next move? Does anybody know what Farrant did when he left the Yard - or what he's doing now?"

Alec moved towards the battery of phones.

"I'll get Records on to it straight away."

"While you're about it," said Gideon, "I'd get Traffic to check on a black Capri - licence number VNP 244P. Though I expect it's been changed by now. Farrant must have known the risk that someone could have spotted the number. In fact he's probably been able to foresee most of the steps we've taken in the case so far. That's the curse of being up against an ex-detective."

137

"I think you might have to withdraw that 'ex', George," said Matt suddenly. "I've just remembered something."

He spoke softly, but with a suppressed excitement that won him the instant attention of everyone in the room. All eyes followed him as he walked to the door, to return after a moment with a Yellow Pages telephone directory taken from the hall table.

He had already found the page he wanted, and pausing only to run the inevitable hand through his tousled hair, he read aloud, " '*DETECTIVES, PRIVATE. The John Farrant Agency. Backed by fifteen years of top-level police experience. Very reasonable rates. All inquiries treated in the strictest confidence. 141 Abbot Hill Drive, Fulham. Telephone* . . .' "

There was a long, stunned silence.

"My God," said Gideon softly. "He's less than a mile away. And Abbot Hill Drive is a residential road, so that address is probably his house as well as his office."

Penny was suddenly standing.

"Do you – do you think that – that George could be there?"

"Steady," said Gideon. "It's far too early to start hoping for something like that."

But he couldn't conceal the fact that at the prospect of action after all these hours of waiting and near-despair, his own spirits were soaring. Rising as abruptly as Penny, he strode across to Matt, snatching the copy of Yellow Pages to see for himself the almost incredible entry.

"The John Farrant Agency, eh?" he said, and actually found himself grinning. "Sounds like just the firm to solve this case for us. I suggest we go and see them straight away . . ."

15 The Swinging Door

It wasn't quite as easy as that. Five minutes of intense planning took place before what amounted to a full-scale police raid on 141 Abbot Hill Drive was prepared.

Matt rang Fulham police station and arranged for a carload of plain clothes men to proceed immediately to the Drive. They were not to approach No. 141 but were to reconnoitre the building and, as unobtrusively as possible, keep watch on all entrances and exits.

The frontal assault, so to speak, was to be carried out by Matt himself, assisted by Gideon and Hobbs. "Just about the most powerful assistance ever given to a Chief Detective Superintendent in police history, I'd say," Matt remarked, with a hint of awe in his voice. It was the only sign he had given that day that he was bothered by his peculiar position in this case – being, in a sense, in charge of the C.I.D.'s Commander and the Assistant Commissioner (Crime)!

He had no reason to be bothered, Gideon thought. He had

not only taken charge, but done so brilliantly – with a humanity, imagination and determination that no one else in the C.I.D. could have equalled.

Who but Matt Honiwell would have dared to suggest that his Commander's wife should undergo hypnosis? And he had not merely suggested it, but gently and firmly *insisted* on it . . . thereby transforming the case, and all their prospects of success.

He was doing some more gentle insisting now. Under no circumstances, he was saying, should Kate or Penny come with them to Abbot Hill Drive. Both turned appealingly to Gideon to override the decision, but that was the last thing he intended to do. There might be trouble, perhaps even shooting – in which case Penny, never far from hysteria today, simply couldn't be guaranteed not to break down. And it would be obvious lunacy, medically, for Kate to be exposed to any more strain and tension than could possibly be helped.

Gideon was about to point out all this, but then he realised that such a painful argument wasn't called for. All he had to do was smile apologetically and say, "I'm sorry, but Matt here's the guv'nor."

There were, he was beginning to realise, certain advantages to a Back Seat Day.

Two minutes later, Gideon was literally in the back seat – of Alec's flashy green Mercedes Benz, which had been brought round from Scotland Yard during the day. Alec himself was at the wheel, with Honiwell beside him.

There was a police radio under the dashboard, and Matt lost no time in establishing contact with the men from Fulham C.I.D., who were at that moment just turning into Abbot Hill Drive.

Their leader, a Detective Inspector Martin, told him, "We

are now passing Number eleven sir. So I imagine Number one four one will be coming up in about half a minute, on the same side of the road, to our left.''

Gideon tensed. They were nearing the moment of truth.

He was under no delusions that bitter disappointment might be lying ahead of them. Small detective agencies were often fly-by-night concerns. It was quite on the cards that they would find the Farrant place long closed and deserted. A new thought struck him. It was an odd coincidence that Farrant's office should be so close to the Hobbs's home. Was it possible that it had been opened there specifically to serve as an operations base for the kidnapping? Now he came to think of it, the crime had shown all the signs of being meticulously organised. For the car to have arrived at exactly the right moment, it looked as though an hour by hour watch had been kept on the house and garden; perhaps there had even been phone-tapping. Farrant, after all, knew all the tricks of the detective's – and the criminal's – trades.

Gideon's heart sank. If the office had been merely an operational H.Q., then obviously it would have been closed down the moment the operation was completed. It was surely most unlikely that Farrant would have taken the baby back there, almost right under the noses of the searching C.I.D.!

Or *was* it so unlikely?

Farrant, after all, had had no reason to suppose that the C.I.D. would suspect him. Despite his dubious record, he was still a detective, and proudly boasted in his advertisement of his ''top-level police experience''. It was entirely possible that during the day someone in the C.I.D. had actually rung him up and asked for his help. It was routine police practice to approach local private eyes and ask them to keep their eyes open, if some big investigation was going on in the vicinity.

141

Yes, Farrant might well have considered his own office to be the safest place in England in which to conceal the baby. And if his own home was above that office, and he had persuaded (or bullied) his wretched wife Jill into being his accomplice, there was, after all, a real possibility that they might find little George there!

Unless – unless Farrant was a psychopath, after all, and had kidnapped merely to kill . . .

Gideon's thoughts, see-sawing dizzily between highest hope and deepest despair, were abruptly interrupted.

Over the radio, Detective Inspector Martin announced, "We're just passing Number one oh nine, sir. One four one should be in the next terrace but one, I reckon."

"Terrace?" said Matt.

"Yes, sir. They are all terraced houses in this street, with small rooms, two up and two down, I'd say, and postage-stamp size gardens in front. Not many garages. Cars mostly parked outside their owners' front doors, all the way down the street. Odd place for a detective agency, but I suppose it wouldn't cost an arm and a leg to set up here . . . "

"We don't need a travelogue, Martin," Honiwell said sharply. "Just tell us if there's any sign of life at Number one four one. And if there is, remember, you drive on past without slowing down – even for a second. Got it?"

"I've got it, sir . . . and we're passing – er, we've *passed* – it now."

There was a short, infuriating, seemingly inexplicable pause, during which nothing but crackles came over the radio.

"Well?" barked Matt. "*Was* there any sign of life?"

The voice of Detective Inspector Martin came back on the air, strangely hesitant now.

"Sorry for that delay, sir. I was just checking with the

others in the car, to make sure they'd seen the same as me. We all agree that there were lights in both the upstairs and downstairs windows – that is, in the front bedroom window and the hall.''

"Great," said Matt. "But why the consultation? I'd have taken the word of any of you on that.''

There was another short pause; another faint, rather ominous crackle.

Then Martin said, "We also all agree that the plate glass in the front door has been smashed, that there is broken glass all over the front garden, and that the front door has been left wide open. In fact, sir, it's swinging to and fro.''

*   *   *

Three minutes later, Matt Honiwell was standing on the glass-strewn steps of No. 141, staring at the door, with Hobbs and Gideon just behind him.

"Let's go in," he said. "It's pretty obvious that there's nobody home.''

He pushed open the door, more glass falling as he did so, this time on to the fitted carpet in the hall - a bright red carpet, with a vivid zigzag pattern that hurt the eyes.

Despite the distracting pattern, Alec spotted something lying on the carpet. He pounced on it, picked it up and held it out. His hand was shaking; it was a moment before he could speak.

A glance at the object told Gideon why.

It was a tiny woollen mouse, blue with pink eyes and gummed-on white whiskers, which Penny's sister had knitted for little George, and which had been in the baby's pram that morning.

There could hardly have been stronger proof that they were

143

hot on the trail, thought Gideon; and a moment later, there
was more. Caught on the catch of the open door was a
fragment of blue wool, exactly the colour of the knitted
matinée coat that George had been wearing. Gideon himself
could testify to that. In this case, it had been Kate who had
done the knitting, and balls of that wool had been a
familiar sight around the house for weeks.

"Seems pretty clear what's happened," said Matt.
"Somebody came down this hall, carrying the baby, and went
out of the house, in too much of a hurry to pick up anything
of the baby's that dropped, or to care if the matinée coat got
ripped. Then, after slamming the door so fiercely that all this
glass got shattered, he (or she) ran on down the path and
drove off with the baby in a car. We know that it would have
been parked just by the gate. There are no garages in the
road."

"But there's nothing wrong with the Yale lock on the
door," said Alec. "If the door was slammed, however
fiercely, it should have locked. Why is it swinging to and fro
now?"

"Somebody must have opened it again," Gideon said.
"Perhaps someone giving chase . . ."

A theory was beginning to form at the back of his mind,
and as they went over No. 141, a lot of things seemed to
confirm it.

The house contained three main rooms: a downstairs
lounge, and two upstairs bedrooms. The lounge had been
converted into an office, and the front upstairs bedroom into a
living room. At the back on the ground floor was a kitchen,
with the remaining bedroom (naturally a double one) above it.

All the rooms except the office showed signs of a violent
struggle. In the bedroom the dressing-table mirror had been

cracked, and all the objects that had been standing in front of it - two bottles of perfume, a hairbrush and several glass ornaments - had been thrown on the floor. In the living room a coffee table had been overturned. In the kitchen there was broken crockery all over the place, and - most sinister of all - a carving knife was found lying on the floor beside the sink, with visible traces of blood on its blade. It didn't look as if anyone had been seriously wounded - in that case, there would have been far more blood about - but someone could have got a nasty nick or slash.

"Not exactly signs of domestic bliss," Gideon said, and suddenly found himself voicing his whole theory. "Look. We know that Farrant bullied his wife, Jill, and kept her under his thumb. Probably he'd made her an unwilling accessory to the kidnapping, and was forcing her to help him with the baby. Suddenly something - perhaps the sight of the helpless newborn baby itself, perhaps the thought of the enormous hue and cry going on - makes her revolt. More than that, it sends her into a violent frenzy. Farrant struggles with her, but for once in his life, can't master her. Somehow - perhaps with a gash from that carving knife   she puts him momentarily out of action. She seizes the opportunity to take off with the baby, slamming the front door behind her. Farrant comes rushing after her, opening the door in the process, but being in such a tearing hurry that he forgets to close it behind him, and leaves it swinging to and fro. Perhaps it was he who broke the glass, by crashing the door back against the wall when he was charging through . . . " Staring round the kitchen, Gideon suddenly changed from detective to concerned grandfather. "There's one thing I'm glad to see, anyway. The Farrants *have* been looking after the baby."

Two cartons of powdered milk (labelled "suitable for

babies") were lying on top of the fridge, with a baby's bottle beside them. Under the draining-board was a bucket of water with two soiled nappies floating in it; from the smell, strong disinfectant, probably Milton, had been added. A packet of freshly-bought nappies lay on the kitchen table, together with a tin of baby powder and even a jar of anti-nappy-rash cream.

The relief in Alec's eyes when he saw these baby products was indescribable.

"Yes. Whatever Farrant was intending, it certainly wasn't harm to George," he said. "That's the same brand of baby powder that Penny uses. Must – " Just for a moment, his voice was near to breaking. "Must have made the poor little mite feel quite a home."

At that moment, Matt came into the room – a smiling Matt, looking almost as relieved as Alec. He had just been questioning the people at the house next door. The man there, a young insurance clerk named Cranston, said that his wife had heard a lot of shouting and screaming at No. 141, but had taken no notice of it; the Farrants were always having rows. Cranston had come to his door, though, when he had heard the crash of falling glass and had been just in time to see Jill Farrant driving off in her husband's Mini Metro. Farrant, looking beside himself with fury, had tried to run after it, but had given up the attempt. When Cranston had last seen him, he had been standing on the pavement, shouting and waving his fists at the red tail-light of the Mini Metro disappearing into the distance. All this had happened at about 9 p.m., just half an hour before.

"So to all intents and purposes," Matt ended, "this case is over. The baby has already been rescued from the kidnapper – by the kidnapper's wife. I imagine that all Jill Farrant is doing now is driving round and round, trying to figure out how to hand back the baby without being spotted. I can soon get the number of the Mini Metro, anyway, and it shouldn't be long before we pull her in."

Matt was planning to leave Detective Inspector Martin and his men to take over at No. 141, while he went on to Fulham to direct the hunt for the Mini Metro – and to try to pull in Farrant himself.

Courteously, he made it clear that he did not want Gideon or Hobbs to accompany him, and Gideon could understand why. It was the personal involvement factor again. The temptation to back-seat drive would become unbearable once the moment of the baby's recovery drew near. And if tricky decisions had to be taken – such as whether or not patrol cars should be diverted from the Whitgate area to Fulham, or whether Jill Farrant should be charged or allowed to go free – he and Alec would be in an impossible position. How in God's name could they pretend that they would be able to make impartial judgments – *or* have the willpower to sit quiet while others made them? Matt was obviously right in feeling that they should keep right away from the scene.

Alec seemed to understand and sympathise with this feeling, too.

"I'll drive you to the station then, Matt," he said, "and after that I'll be on standby at home. I ought to go there, anyway. Scott-Marle wants me to ring him at ten about the Whitgate crisis, and I'm dying to see Penny's face when I tell her the good news. Coming, George?"

Gideon shook his head.

"Not just for the moment. There's a little more looking round I'd like to do here," he said. "Tell Kate I won't be long. One of Martin's men can run me back when I'm through."

He tried to keep his voice brisk and cheerful, as though he shared the general confidence that the case was as good as over, and that the baby would soon be found. Inwardly, he was full of misgivings.

Why had Farrant not returned to No. 141 once he had realised that Jill had got away? It looked as if he had rushed off to start a search for his wife on his own account. It was not pleasant to think what might happen if he found her before the police did. He must be dangerously angry by now, and had probably been drinking, too. Drink had been one of Farrant's great weaknesses . . .

And as for Jill Farrant - was she really "driving round and round, trying to figure out how to hand back the baby" - or was that just cuddly Matt's natural optimism? All they knew for certain was that she was in a pretty distraught state, following a savage struggle. The thought of a girl in such a state being behind the wheel of a car - with little George on her lap, or on the seat beside her - was nothing short of terrifying.

To force it out of his mind, Gideon compelled himself to concentrate on the baffling central enigma of the case. Just what had Farrant been trying to achieve? Why, why, *why* should a man with an overriding ambition and a limitless capacity for calculation have kidnapped a baby which he couldn't possibly keep, wouldn't dare to hold to ransom and - thank God - seemingly didn't intend to kill?

There had to be an answer - and the most likely place to find it was in the room they had hardly searched: the downstairs lounge which had been converted into the office of The John Farrant Agency.

As soon as Alec and Matt had gone, leaving Detective Inspector Martin and his plain-clothes men in charge of the house, Gideon marched into the Farrant office and began going through drawers and opening filing cabinets.

Martin and a Detective Sergeant stood in the doorway, watching. Martin, a grey-haired man in his late fifties, rather slightly built for a copper, looked excited and overawed at the thought of being in such close proximity to the great Gideon. The Detective Sergeant, on the other hand, kept throwing surreptitious glances at his watch, as if wondering when the hell someone would decide it was time to knock off. Gideon glowered at him, but then thought that he was probably one of the C.I.D. men hurriedly roped in from other areas to help with the kidnapping emergency. In which case, he might well have been on duty for twelve hours or more, and was feeling dead on his feet.

Gideon's guess was right. The man in question had started that morning at nine, and although it had begun lazily, he had had a day with enough nervous tension in it to last him a lifetime. It was Detective Sergeant Potter from Pimlico.

"Can we be of any help to you, sir?" Martin asked nervously. "If you could give us a rough idea of what you're looking for . . ."

"I should have thought that was fairly obvious," Gideon snapped. "I'm looking for a *reason*, Martin."

"You mean – a reason why Farrant should have carried out the snatch, sir?"

Gideon almost groaned aloud.

As he had shown during his meticulous running commentary from the police car – never reporting an observation until all his men had confirmed seeing the same thing – Detective Inspector Martin had one of those punctilious, cautious minds that moved forward inch by inch, like a man stepping across floorboards he feared to be rotten. Such minds were all too common in the C.I.D., and Gideon had yet to hear any of their owners come up with anything original or constructive.

As if sensing from Gideon's expression how little was hoped for from him, Martin relapsed into silence; but he came into the room, and joined Gideon in searching through filing cabinets and drawers. Nothing much was gained from them, except pathetic evidence of how badly the Farrant agency was doing. Cabinet after cabinet contained nothing but empty files. It hardly looked as if any inquiries were currently proceeding at all.

At last, Martin spoke – and immediately wished he hadn't.

"I suppose Farrant couldn't have kidnapped the baby in order to give himself a case, sir – and boost his agency?"

"What?"

Gideon slammed shut the bottom drawer of a particularly massive metal cabinet.

"For Heaven's sake, Martin, if all you can do is make preposterous suggestions – "

He broke off in mid-sentence, thinking furiously. An outstanding success, like the recovery of the Assistant Commissioner's own baby, would certainly transform the Farrant Agency's prospects. And for an experienced evidence-faker, it would not be too difficult to make it appear that the kidnapping had been carried out by some unknown enemy, who had been defeated by the brilliance and astuteness of one John Farrant.

"I am sorry the criminals got away," he could imagine Farrant saying in his ingratiating way, "but fortunately, our operators were successful in rescuing the baby – and here he is, Commander Gideon, absolutely safe and sound. No, of course there'll be no charge. The John Farrant Agency is only too happy to be of some small service to the Metropolitan Police.

150

Though of course, we'd have no objection if, in the future, you put the odd bit of business our way.''

Not that he'd need the police to put business his way. There would be Farrant headlines in all the national newspapers, Farrant interviews on radio and TV. At the cost of a single risky operation, Farrant would have earned himself a million pounds' worth of publicity. He would have put himself back on the way to the top, satisfied that pathological need to please – and at the same time, wreaked a sneaky revenge by inflicting hours of intense anxiety on him, Gideon . . . to say nothing of what he had done to Kate.

The more Gideon thought about it, the less preposterous Martin's suggestion seemed. His opinion about the Detective Inspector's mental ability changed rapidly – and being Gideon, he did not hesitate to say so.

"It's a hard world, Martin," he grunted. "You come up with a brilliantly shrewd answer to my question, and all I do is snap your head off.''

Martin stared blankly. It took seconds for his cautious mind to allow him to accept that he was actually being complimented by the Commander of the C.I.D. When the truth did dawn, he reddened all the way from his cheekbones to his chin.

"It was only an off-the-cuff suggestion, sir. I may be entirely mistaken.''

"We can soon prove it, one way or the other," Gideon said, looking around him. "If Farrant is planning to make himself out to be a rescuing hero, he's bound to have prepared his ground. There will be details of a phony investigation hidden away somewhere – and I would guess that that somewhere is here!''

He and Martin began searching the room again, now with

renewed fervour. They took the drawers out of the desk and the filing cabinets, removed their contents and tapped them all round in search of hidden compartments. The drawer from one filing cabinet seemed suspiciously heavier than its fellows. Gideon fumbled with it for several seconds, then found a secret spring. The metal at the base opened like a hinged door, and a thick file was revealed, whose title was self-explanatory.

THE HOBBS KIDNAPPING

One of the sheets inside was obviously the rough draft of a press handout. It began:

"It was 14.25 when the Agency first received news that the 10-day-old baby of Deputy Commander shortly to be Assistant Commissioner Alec Hobbs had been kidnapped from the Hobbs's garden, not a mile from the Agency's front door!"

Then came elaborate details of underworld figures contacted, and of other leads that had allegedly been followed. Finally there was a stirring account of how Farrant himself, following an anonymous tip-off, chased and caught up with the kidnappers in their black Ford Capri, held them up at gunpoint, and recovered the baby at great personal risk. The kidnappers themselves escaped because – a very clever touch this, Gideon thought – with the infant in his arms, Farrant could no longer effectively cover them with his gun!

Farrant had apparently planned to stage the dramatic rescue scene on the other side of the Thames, on a desolate stretch of Barnes Common, at 10 p.m.

"In other words," said Gideon, looking at his watch, "it would have happened half an hour ago . . . but for the fact that Mrs. Farrant had already decided to stage her own rescue scene."

Rescue scene?

Gideon frowned uneasily.

It didn't make sense any more to talk of Jill Farrant rescuing little George. She must have known that Farrant meant him no harm and was, in fact, on the point of returning him, in his own devious way.

Why, then, should she have dashed off with the baby herself?

And more important – *where could she be taking him?*

The signs of violence around the house – the bloodstained knife in the kitchen, the damaged dressing table in the bedroom, the smashed glass in the front door – suggested that Jill had been in something more than just a fury. It looked as if she had gone completely berserk, suddenly hitting back against her husband with everything she'd got, and savagely wrecking all his plans in an explosion of hysterical frenzy.

Who could hazard a guess at her intentions now? She probably didn't know them herself. She was most likely simply batting on through the night, at God knew what speed, hardly hearing the baby crying, scarcely aware of anything except her own all-engulfing hate.

Gideon didn't say any of this aloud, but the surprisingly shrewd Martin had no trouble divining from his expression what he was thinking.

"Don't ask me to suggest a reason for *Mrs.* Farrant's behaviour," he said fervently. "The ways of women have always been beyond me."

Suddenly, Detective-Sergeant Potter spoke up for the first time. Up till now, he had been standing rather stupidly in a corner, battling, Gideon had thought, with tiredness or boredom or both, but in any event, clearly following that old, old precept of bad policemen, "do nothing until told what to do".

153

It seemed, though, that Martin's remark had woken him up at last.

"They're beyond me, too," he said.

And not knowing quite why he was doing it, driven by some odd, inexplicable hunch that this was something Commander Gideon ought to know, Potter launched out on a description of how, in Pimlico that morning, a girl had gone into screaming hysterics at the sight of a child's rubber ball.

16   The Bouncing Ball

Gideon was hardly listening at first. Potter had not impressed
him. Admittedly the man might be tired, but that hardly
excused his totally negative attitude over the past half hour.
He had better things to do, Gideon told himself, than waste
his time on idle chatter from an idle man.

But the sheer intensity with which Potter began his story
made it impossible for Gideon to ignore what he was saying.
And suddenly a sentence riveted his attention.

"*There I was in the stake-out watching the shop, when I heard
this scream –* "

"A stake-out?"

In a flash, Gideon had strode across to Potter, and was
towering over him.

"This shop you were watching – was it the Swanleigh's?"

"Why, yes, sir."

Potter's tone registered astonishment that the Commander
of the C.I.D. should be able to remember the details of what

he thought of as a minor murder inquiry. In that case, Gideon thought grimly, he had a few more surprises in store for him.

"The girl who screamed – was it Anne Swanleigh?"

"Yes, sir. I rushed across to the shop, of course, thinking she was being attacked."

"You'd seen someone go in?"

"Er – well, no, but I might have missed it. No one's infallible, sir."

Gideon noticed that Potter was sweating. Obviously he hadn't been watching the shop too carefully. But it had been a hot morning; the surveillance *had* proved fruitless for thirteen weeks . . . He decided not to press the point further.

"When you reached the shop, what did you find?"

"Nothing, sir. Absolutely nothing that could have caused any normal person to scream out like that. But there was Anne Swanleigh, in a state of total terror, staring at a rubber ball that had accidentally bounced off a plastic rack behind the counter."

"Did she say why the ball had frightened her so much?"

"No, sir. She just said it seemed to remind her of something, but she didn't know what. I thought some memory of the man who had attacked her might be coming back. Er – you may think it was unwise, sir, but I tried a psychological experiment."

Gideon raised an eyebrow. So this Potter *could* show initiative at times.

"Oh, you did, did you?" he said.

"Yes, sir. I took the ball, and threw it up in the air. But when it came down, I missed it, and the moment she saw it bouncing round the shop, Anne Swanleigh started screaming again – louder, if anything, than before."

"What happened then?"

156

"Her invalid father started calling out from the room at the back, and she went rushing in to him, sobbing. I went back to the stake-out, pretty scared myself. I was afraid my psychological blundering might have unbalanced the girl's mind."

Gideon's expression softened. Potter might be idle and incompetent, but at least he wasn't callous, and he was prepared to question and worry about his own actions, which was rare amongst young C.I.D. men these days. Perhaps there was more to it than that. Perhaps his mind hadn't been on the kidnapping *because* it was still haunted by what had happened at the Swanleigh shop. Harrowing cases like that could get under the most unlikely person's skin.

Aloud, he said, "Don't blame yourself too much, Potter. I may have done far more to endanger that girl than you. It was I who ordered the stake-out to be closed down this afternoon. Do you happen to know how she and her father took that news?"

"No, sir. As soon as it was shut, I was ordered to come here. Chief Detective Superintendent Price went to explain the position to the Swanleighs, I believe, before he left for Whitgate to help in the emergency there."

"But he'll be round at the Swanleighs as soon as he's off duty," Gideon mused. "I suspect he's on very friendly terms with that family."

Potter was staring at him now with something approaching awe.

"You don't miss much, sir, do you?"

Gideon did not feel he deserved the compliment tonight. He had missed the whole motive behind the kidnapping of the baby, and he had an uneasy feeling that now he was missing something else, failing to spot a vital clue that was staring him in the face in this business of the bouncing ball.

157

Suddenly – for the first time in twelve hours – he remembered the video cassette which he had almost thrown into the wastebin, but which he had pocketed on a sudden hunch.

He felt in his jacket pocket, found the cassette, and held it so that Potter could see it.

"It's a 'scene of the crime simulation' tape," he said. "Made after the murder of Anne Swanleigh's mother, three months ago."

As he spoke, that hunch he had had about the cassette returned with doubled force. It was now an irresistible, unquestionable command.

"Potter. Can you drive that police car outside?"

"Yes, of course, sir."

"Then take me to the Assistant Commissioner's house. Fast. There'll be equipment there on which we can view this cassette – and I've a feeling it's something that both you and I urgently need to see."

Ordering a rather baffled Martin to stay at the house, he led the way out to the car.

*　　　*　　　*

The cassette was not the only thing that Gideon took with him to the Hobbs's. He also brought Farrant's secret file.

As he looked through it, Alec was at first uncomprehending, then incredulous – and finally almost overcome with relief.

"So the whole time, little George has never been in any real danger," he said.

It was on the tip of Gideon's tongue to add, "Until now." But he thought better of it, and instead asked, "Has there been any word from Matt at Fulham?"

"No. But he's set up roadblocks, and has a fleet of Pandas out patrolling the streets. I don't think it'll be any time before Jill Farrant's pulled in. Do you?"

Gideon managed a noncommittal grunt. There was no point in revealing his forebodings, and perhaps they were irrational anyway. The point was that a confident Alec would spread his mood to Penny and Kate, and it wouldn't do any harm for them to feel relaxed and happier for a while, whether or not they were wholly justified in doing so.

"To tell you the truth," Alec continued, dropping his voice to a confidential level, "I'm far more concerned at the moment about the Whitgate situation. Scott-Marle is on tenterhooks, and so is the Home Secretary. We're sending more and more men into the area – both Uniform and C.I.D. – and believe it or not, Scott-Marle has authorised me to arm nearly all of them."

Gideon whistled. "You're really expecting a shoot-out?"

Lemaitre's words from that morning suddenly seemed to be ringing in his ears. "Somebody's trying to start a civil war." Was that actually occurring?

They were in Alec's study, which still looked like (and was actually in use as) a police H.Q. The big boardroom-style table with its mass of telephones left little room for pacing, but nevertheless Alec was walking restlessly up and down.

"I don't know what I'm expecting. Special Branch has had a tip-off that both the BGBM and the WUW have big armouries somewhere in the area. About an hour ago, Lem sent Derek Price with a C.I.D. team on a house to house hunt for weapons, involving calls on all known activists in both parties. But so far they haven't found a single gun – nor, for that matter, anybody home."

Which meant, Gideon thought, that there could be dozens

of political fanatics on the streets of Whitgate, equipped with loaded guns from the unknown armouries. There was no easy way of catching them. Even a series of spot checks could be dangerous, with both the police and the people they questioned possessing guns.

"Is Lem still holding the two leaders, Caxton and what's-his-name – er, Major Strode?"

"I think so. God knows if he's got any sense out of them."

"What about the stretch of High Street outside the police station? Is it still quiet?"

"So far. But it's filling up with people. And the word going round is that midnight's the danger time."

Gideon glanced at his watch – which said 11.07.

"Fifty-three minutes to go," he thought, and had a sudden nightmare feeling that for a lot of people, all over London, time could be running out. His mind was suddenly a kaleidoscope of whirling faces, from Farrant's to the baby George's; from Anne Swanleigh's to Lemaitre's; from Jill Farrant's to Kate's. Somewhere in the background a hundred mindless yobbos pointed loaded revolvers. Superimposed were a dozen bouncing rubber balls.

He was tired, of course, that was the trouble. He doubted if he had ever known a day which had exacted quite such a nervous and emotional toll.

There was only one way to restore order to the chaos – that old trick he had learnt of forcing his thinking into watertight compartments. He had to concentrate – fiercely and to the absolute exclusion of everything else – *on one case at a time.*

He suddenly remembered Potter standing beside him, and took the Swanleigh tape from his pocket. He put it into Alec's hands.

160

"Could you give us a showing of this?" he asked. "It could be very important."

Alec glanced at it – then grinned with surprise and delight.

"Well, well. You're showing support for my new techniques at last! This was one of the very earliest of my scene-of-the-crime simulations. I made the tape myself, down at the Swanleigh shop just the day after poor Dorothy Swanleigh's murder. A woman police constable took the part of Dorothy, and Derek Price was the killer. I can't honestly say that the exercise contributed a lot to the inquiry at the time – but it wasn't for want of trying. We not only taped the thing on the exact spot where the killing had taken place, I also went to a lot of pains to ensure that every detail of the surroundings was as correct as possible, no matter how irrelevant it might seem. At the time of the murder, for example, a calendar at the back of the shop had been hanging crooked, on only one drawing pin. It had fallen down since, but I insisted on putting it back up for the purpose of the film. There's another thing I remember." Alec was walking across his study and slipping the cassette into a video recorder on top of a TV set in the corner. "When the body was found, there had been a rubber ball rolling about on the floor of the shop. People kept tripping over it, and it had been put back on the rack behind the counter. But before we started filming, I got it down again and put it on the floor. You can spot it, if you look closely, on the left of the screen at the start of the simulation. See? There . . ."

The screen of the TV had sprung to life. It showed the inside of a small, rather dingy-looking confectioner's and tobacconist's shop with a policewoman in uniform standing behind the counter. (Hobbs had not carried his obsession with detail to the point of making her wear the clothes of the deceased.) The rubber ball was, in fact, clearly visible on the

161

left, lying in front of a stand displaying bags of toffees and chocolates. The rack which the ball had come from was just behind the policewoman. It stood next to an open door at the back of the counter; the door, Gideon remembered, that led to the little back room where Reginald Swanleigh had sat, hearing his wife's screams but tragically powerless to help her. There was one curious fact that had already struck him. The counter was a high one, a good four feet off the floor. There was, therefore, no possibility that the ball could have *bounced* off the rack and over the counter. Someone must have deliberately thrown it over on to the floor of the shop.

"Do you remember if a similar ball was found rolling around the floor of the shop after Anne Swanleigh was attacked?" Gideon asked.

"I rather think there was," said Alec. "I remember Price saying that there must be something faulty about the rack. Why? Is it important?"

"Yes. Vital," Gideon said.

On the screen, the shop door opened, with the accompanying *ping* of a bell, and Derek Price entered in the role of murderer. With his heavy build, he looked powerful enough for the part, Gideon thought. As he passed the video camera, it could be seen that he was holding a heavy clawhammer raised in his hand. He struck her once. She screamed several times. He struck her again – and she fell.

"What is it, love? What is it? I – Ahhhh . . . "

"That was me again, as Reggie Swanleigh," Alec said. "Though I'm afraid it was really beyond me to mimic the sound of a paralysed man, so terrified that he actually manages to get out of his chair – and then falls unconscious." The screen went dark. "Well, that's the end of the simulation. Do you want to see it again?"

162

"No," said Gideon. "But I would like a few questions about it answered. I don't remember anything in Reggie Swanleigh's statement about him calling out to Dorothy just before the murderer struck."

"True," said Alec. "But the old boy's memories were very confused. And I realised that something like that must have happened. Why else should the wounds have been on the *back* of Dorothy's head?"

"Why indeed?" said Gideon softly. He was suddenly standing, his face very grave and tense. "Correct me if I'm wrong . . . but surely when Anne Swanleigh was attacked, her wounds were also at the back of the head."

"That's right," Alec said. "Price and I assumed that on the second occasion, the killer employed some trick - he probably asked Anne to fetch something from a shelf behind the counter, so that she would turn her head away and not see the blow coming until it was too late."

"A girl who is terrified that any customer may be a killer," said Gideon slowly, "isn't going to turn her back for more than a second on anyone. I doubt if that would have given him time."

Alec came near to losing his temper.

"Well, there are only two possible conclusions," he snapped. "Either something made both Dorothy and Anne Swanleigh turn their heads - or else the killer came up behind them, through the door at the back of the counter. But behind that door is the room where Reggie was sitting. It's conceivable that the killer was someone he knew well, and allowed to pass him - the first time. But why didn't he mention it afterwards? And surely to God, there's no way he could have allowed it to happen twice."

"No," said Gideon, and suddenly his face was very grave,

163

and his voice very slow. "So if in fact the killer did come through that door, there's only one person he could have been. *Reggie Swanleigh himself.*"

Both Alec and Potter stared at him as if he had gone mad.

"A pathetic old boy paralysed from the neck down and not able even to propel himself about in a wheelchair?" Alec said.

Gideon swallowed hard. He didn't blame them for being shaken. He was as startled as they were at the direction his thoughts were taking. But he couldn't stop now. For the sake of everyone, not least Anne Swanleigh, he had to explore every possibility – however hideous.

"He is able, we know, to spring right out of that chair under extreme provocation," he reminded them. "How can we be sure that his wife and daughter didn't give him just that? Not intentionally, of course. But being locked in a wheelchair can do strange things to some minds. With nothing to do but sit and brood, old jealousies and suspicions can build up into manias. We know that twenty years before, Dorothy had gone off with a man called Anthony Marsden . . . and Anne Swanleigh is around twenty years old. Supposing Reggie got the idea into his head that his wife had been deceiving him about Anne, and that she was Marsden's daughter and not his?"

"I can remember something that may give strength to that, sir," Potter suddenly said. "I overheard a remark he made to Anne, after she'd broken down, screaming, in the shop. 'Try to act like my daughter,' he said. I didn't take much notice of it at the time, but looking back, it seems to suggest that he may have had suspicions about her."

"And suspicions like that could have driven him into a murderous fury against both the girl and her mother," said

Gideon. "A fury so strong that it broke through the paralysis, and – "

"Sorry, George," Alec interrupted. "But I just can't buy this, and I'll tell you why. Even if he could overcome his paralysis and get out of the wheelchair, Swanleigh still wouldn't have been able to move like a normal man. He'd be heavy-footed, clumsy, blundering, even if very strong. How could he possibly have got through that door behind the counter and crept up on them without their hearing something and looking round? Unless, of course, he somehow distracted their attention."

"But that's exactly what he did do," said Gideon. "He picked up a ball from the rack just inside the door, and threw it across the counter so that it bounced all over the shop."

His voice was now so tense that it was little more than a whisper.

"Can you imagine anything more distracting than the sudden appearance, from nowhere, of a bouncing rubber ball?"

165

17   The Only Hope

There was a long, shocked silence in the room.

Then the flood of objections began.

"But after the murder of his wife, Reggie Swanleigh was found completely unconscious, presumably from overstraining his paralysed muscles with that one leap out of his chair," said Alec. "That was what the doctor concluded, anyway."

"But he also said that what had happened was almost a medical impossibility," Gideon snapped. "So why not allow a few more medical impossibilities? Swanleigh may not have collapsed getting out of his chair, but *on returning to it.*" His voice became gruffer, grimmer. "And no wonder. I'm surprised the horror of what he'd done didn't kill him."

"But where could he have got the weapon from?"

"There are usually hammers around at the back of shops – for banging up display material, opening crates of purchased goods, and so on. I don't suppose the Swanleigh shop was any exception.''

"How did he get rid of the thing afterwards?''

"He probably hid it somewhere in that back room, perhaps even took it outside and pitched it into a dustbin. He could have disposed of a bloodstained coat in the same way. We'll never know – because of course it never entered anyone's mind to search any part of the premises except the shop. Total paralysis is a total alibi. But when even doctors admit that a paralysis *isn't* total – well, it must raise questions about the alibi too.''

Potter raised the next objection.

"From what I've heard, sir, Swanleigh was always begging Mr. Price *not* to close down that stake-out. If he was the killer, and was planning to attack Anne again . . . ''

"I don't think there was much planning about the attacks,'' Gideon said. "They were probably much more like mental seizures, perhaps only dimly remembered afterwards. In that case what Swanleigh was really begging for was *police protection for his daughter - from himself.* It is protection that was obviously desperately urgently needed.'' Slowly, significantly, he corrected himself. "*Is* desperately urgently needed. And the most worrying thing is that, thanks to me, for a full seven hours there has been none at all.''

There was nothing slow about his movements as he crossed to the big boardroom table and picked up a phone. Potter imagined that he was going to ring some Scotland Yard department, and was astonished when he suddenly turned to him and barked:

"Potter, do you happen to know the Swanleighs' telephone number?''

Potter had a notebook with him, and hastily consulted it.

167

The number was there, under the address of the Swanleigh shop.

He read it out to Gideon, who started dialling as soon as he heard the first digit.

Another silence fell on the room, a silence so intense that the ringing tone was almost as audible to Hobbs and Potter as it was to Gideon. And there was the same expression of anxiety on all their faces as the ringing tone went on. And on. And on.

"Anne Swanleigh *must* be there," Potter breathed. "She never goes out day or night, I've heard, except for the couple of hours when the district nurse calls."

Alec leant forward tensely.

"What you're saying is that if she *doesn't* answer, that can only mean that the Commander's right."

"Not necessarily," said Gideon sharply. Rarely in his life had he so wanted to be proved wrong. "A lot of other things could be keeping her from the telephone. She could be helping her father get to bed. She could be taking a bath. She could be – "

He broke off, silenced by what he knew they were both thinking.

She could be lying dead.

And if she were, it would be all because he had refused to listen to Derek Price's hunches – even though they'd been echoed by his own.

Price, he thought, might be the man to approach now. If he could be reached at Whitgate police station, and Lemaitre agreed to release him, he could cover the two miles between Whitgate and Pimlico in a matter of minutes. He'd probably get there sooner than anyone from Pimlico police station could.

He only hoped he wouldn't be sending Price on a journey that would end with the discovery of . . .

Gideon wouldn't let his brain finish the thought.

He silenced the endless ringing tone by depressing the receiver rest with his forefinger, and then hastily dialled the Whitgate police station number. There was no need for him to look it up. He knew the numbers of all the police stations in Central London off by heart.

He asked to be put straight through to the Divisional Superintendent, and a couple of seconds later, he heard the familiar Cockney tones of Lemaitre.

"Gee Gee, thank God it's you! Listen. I'm in dead trouble here, and I really need your advice. The situation is - "

"Whatever the situation is, it can wait," Gideon thundered. "At least till I've had a chance to speak to Derek Price. Is he there?"

"Price?" Lemaitre seemed surprised. "Yes, he's here. He's been worth his weight in gold to me, with all the help he's been giving. He was directing a house to house weapons search, but we've just called it off. Results: total zero. That's one of the most worrying things - "

"For God's sake, Lem, shut up and *let me talk to Price!*"

It was a full-scale Gideon roar, and it took Lem back to the years he had spent as Gideon's second in command, during which he had heard it almost every day. Yet familiarity had not lessened its power to make him gasp.

"Yes. Right. At once, Gee Gee," he said, in three startled yelps, and, in less than a second, Price was on the line sounding equally startled, and closer to stammering than ever.

"P-P-Price here, sir. Is-is it something about Anne?"

It was almost like telepathy, thought Gideon, almost as

169

though something was already telling Price that his hunches were about to be proved hideously right. But that didn't make it any easier to spell out his theory. For the first time in his life, Gideon found *himself* nearly stammering before he was through. To tell a man that the girl he loved was in mortal danger from her own father . . . and that she might alread . . .

Gideon expected stammered arguments and expostulations, or worse, a stunned silence of disbelief.

But Price made no attempt to argue. There was no arguing with that memory, still agonisingly fresh in his mind, of Swanleigh nearly fainting when he had held that rubber ball under his eyes.

Price did not stammer, either.

As always when he really had to, he spoke with startling clarity.

"I'm on my way, sir," he said simply. "Please pray I'm in time."

Gideon tried to reply. But at the thought of what he privately expected Price to find at the end of the journey, not even a grunt would come.

*   *   *

As Price left, Lemaitre was suddenly back on the line, and this time there was no stopping him.

He gave Gideon a tense, rapid-fire recapitulation of the day's events at Whitgate: the sickening parade of pot-shot incidents; the C.I.D. operation, suggested by Gideon and headed by Price, which had ended with virtually all the pot-shooters being rounded up; the shooting of Sir Gilbert Fordyce, apparently by a stray pot-shooter; the lynch fever which had gripped the crowd, and been halted by the arrests of both Jeremy Caxton and Major Strode; the quiet that had prevailed since, with the disturbing rumours that guns were being issued to both sides, and that midnight was going to be Whitgate's High Noon. Now crowds were beginning to build up outside the police station, making Lem feel that the place was almost in a state of siege.

"I know what I should do, according to the copper's manual," Lem said. "I should make arrests, then clear and cordon off the street. I also know what I should do politically – let both the leaders go free, with orders to calm their supporters, or else! But I'm not doing any of those things, Gee Gee, and I'll tell you why. Any police action at all could start bullets flying. And that goes for political actions too. Jeremy Caxton's only got to be seen on the police station steps for a BGBM man to take a shot at him – to avenge their leader. Strode has only got to appear for the Workers lot to have a go – because *his* men tried to lynch Caxton a couple of hours ago. If I try to smuggle them out by the back exit, they've still got to get into cars, and the cars will be fired at as they drive away. And once one shot is fired, in the atmosphere out there, it'll be like a lighted match in a tank of petrol."

"You're almost making out a case for bringing in the Army," Gideon said.

Lem, who knew Gideon better than almost anyone, could guess what it had cost him to say that. To Gideon, calling in the military to do a police job – in the heart of the Metropolitan area – would constitute the greatest personal defeat of his career. He didn't want to involve his old friend in that.

"Blimey, this lot wouldn't turn a hair if you brought in the whole Tank Corps!" he said, and then suddenly his voice became pleading. "There is one thing that I reckon *would* shake them, though. Commander Gideon in person, assuring them that the assassination wasn't political. That it was just another piece of mindless pot-shooting.''

"But was it, Lem?" Gideon asked. "I gather some pretty skilled marksmanship was displayed by the assassin. Supposing . . . ''

But Lem didn't seem to hear. Perhaps he didn't want to.

"If you could tell them about the man deliberately handing out guns to subnormal yobbos – and I'll get Detective Sergeant Blake to stand beside you and tell his cinema story – the mob might just begin to feel that they're behaving like subnormal yobbos themselves.''

"It might work," said Gideon cautiously. "But why me? Why don't you do the job yourself?''

"Talking to crowds isn't my scene," Lem said. "The moment I open my mouth, they'd be using my teeth for target practice. But in thirty years, I've never known a mob *you* couldn't handle . . . ''

Gideon had the gravest doubts about whether he could handle this one, or whether Lem's method was the way to do it. But it was obvious that he had become Lem's only hope. And that meant that he was also London's only hope of being saved from one of the ugliest nights in its history.

"Okay, Lem," he said. "I'll be with you, and we'll sort something out. Yes, before midnight, if I possibly can . . . ''

He replaced the receiver, then glanced at his watch. 11.27. Only thirty-three minutes to go.

A sudden thought struck him, unwelcome as it was unfamiliar. He should have consulted Hobbs before agreeing with Lemaitre on how to handle a major crisis such as this.

He glanced across at Alec, but he was busy on another phone, and when, a couple of seconds later, he replaced *his* receiver, it was obvious that he wanted to talk, not listen.

172

"That was Barnaby, ringing from the Yard. Farrant's been picked up. He was blind drunk, and belting down the Edgware Road at ninety miles an hour. In, incidentally, a black Ford Capri . . . "

18 No Lights

"Has he said anything about Jill Farrant or the baby?"

"No. But he will when I talk to him."

Hobbs was already on his way to the door. At the prospect of coming face to face with the kidnapper of his son, he had completely changed, and was a Hobbs Gideon had never seen, or even glimpsed, before. His face was as flushed and his forehead as damp as if he had just come out of a sauna. His eyes were blazing. His mouth had tightened into a ruler-straight line. It was as though all the smoothness and polish had been blasted off him, leaving a red-hot core of anger. Woe betide anyone who brought up the personal involvement question now!

"Where is he?" Gideon asked.

"He was taken in at Bow Street, but Barnaby's had him brought to the Yard for us to question him. Barnaby's ringing Matt, so by now he will be on his way there too. Coming?"

Gideon hesitated, remembering his promise to Lem to be at Whitgate police station by midnight. But the Yard was on the

174

way there, and his desire to see Farrant – if only for two or three minutes – was as fervent as Hobbs's.

After a word with Penny and Kate to tell them the encouraging news (if it could be called encouraging – Gideon still wasn't sure) Gideon and Hobbs climbed into the Mercedes, with Hobbs taking the wheel.

Potter had been sent to rejoin Martin's C.I.D. team at the Farrant Agency. They would be a team of dead-tired men by now, thought Gideon, but the finding of Farrant would probably mean that they could knock off for the night.

His, Gideon's, night on the other hand was just beginning – a night, he felt in his bones, that would tax all his resources, mental and physical, if his family was to be saved from tragedy, Whitgate from the unthinkable, and London from disaster.

Well, at least there was one thing. It wouldn't be a back-seat night, Gideon told himself, as Alec let in the clutch and the Mercedes roared away from the kerb.

* * *

At almost exactly that moment, four miles away to the north, a police car with its sirens wailing drew up to the kerb outside the Swanleigh shop, and Derek Price got out.

A driver and two other men from Uniform were in the car, but he told them all to stay there.

They did not question his order; they did not, in fact, say anything at all. They were men from the Whitgate police station, and knew nothing about the Swanleigh murder, which they regarded as a Pimlico affair. But they could all sense that this was no ordinary case; that they had come from the strange tensions building up at Whitgate to a spot where even stranger things were in the air. One look at Price was enough to tell them that. He was not behaving remotely like a Chief Detective Superintendent investigating a major case. He was standing motionless on the pavement, with the car door still open behind him, staring at the shop as if turned into a statue. With his heavy build and thrusting jaw, it could have been a statue of the young Winston Churchill.

"No - no lights," he said stumblingly. "Not a single - single one. Any-anywhere in the house."

"Well, it *has* turned half eleven, sir," remarked the driver. "Couldn't the folk here have gone to bed?"

It was, Price supposed, just possible that they had. Anne usually helped her father to go to bed at ten. Knowing that he, Price, was deeply involved at Whitgate, she just might have gone to bed herself, deciding that it wasn't worth waiting up.

But it was a faint hope, as he well knew. Anne always waited up, either downstairs or in the bedroom, if there was the slightest chance that he would come. The windows of both rooms were visible from where he was standing, and both were dark blank squares, reflecting nothing but a few dim stars and the strange orange glow that the myriad street lamps of the Metropolis always gave to the London sky at night.

Faint though the hope was, it restored life to Price's panic-frozen muscles. A second later, he was across the pavement and in the doorway of the shop. Through the intense but slightly orange-tinted darkness, he could just make out a card hanging behind the glass of the shop door. It was one of those cards with "OPEN" on one side and "CLOSED" on the other; and it looked as though it still said "OPEN". Which was strange, because Anne was most punctilious about changing it round.

He tried the door, and sure enough, it was unlocked. There was a loud, eerily echoing *ping* from the overhead doorbell as he opened it wide, but he hardly heard the sound. It was almost drowned by the hammering of his heart and the roaring in his ears, as his brain struggled to cope with an explosion of near-hysterical fears.

The shop – a small, struggling business heavily dependent on after-hours trade – sometimes closed as late as half past eight, but never later. It would have been still light when it shut. It looked as if something had happened to Anne while the shop was still open, and before any lights had been turned on, something so terrible that there had been nothing but silence and darkness since.

Next moment – the worst moment of his life – Price had the grimmest indication of what that something could have been. He took a cautious step forward, and almost tripped over a rubber ball, lying on the floor just by the door.

He tried to pick it up, but his sweaty hands could get no grip on it, and it went bouncing away into the darkness, taking with it every vestige of hope, leaving his whole being, his whole world, cold, dark, empty and dead.

He groped his way forward through the blackness until his fingers brushed against the top of the counter. He ran his hands along it in search of the flap. Behind the counter, there would be light switches; but he needed no telling that they were not all he was likely to find there.

If Anne's father had crept up and struck her down when she had been working in the shop, then that was where she would have fallen. Perhaps that was where her father had fallen too, if the act of killing had had the same effect on him as before, and made him lose consciousness. It was a gruesome scenario, but what else would explain the facts: the "OPEN" sign, the

177

unlocked door, the unlit shop, the unanswered phone, the silent house . . . and the presence of that abominable ball on the floor?

Price had found the counter flap now. He raised it, and tried to grope his way forwards. But the thought of what, at any second, his feet or fingers might encounter robbed him of all power of movement. It was not so much a fear as a fever, making all his limbs weak and trembling, filling his stomach with what felt like molten lead, and covering his face, his neck, his armpits and even his back with rivulets of icy sweat.

It was then that he heard breathing - faint, tortured, irregular - coming from somewhere just below him . . . but the darkness there, in the shadow of the counter, was so intense that his eyes could make out nothing.

Lights, he thought. Now there *had* to be lights . . .

Suddenly he could not only move, he could hurl himself forward. Before he knew it, he was over by the back wall behind the counter, his shaking fingers groping along the light switches.

Then he froze again, this time not in terror, but in an ecstacy of relief, the greatest relief that he had ever known.

"*Don't!*" came Anne's voice, from just below him. "For God's sake, darling, *don't switch them on.*"

*   *   *

The voice sounded hoarse and strained, but not like someone in pain or dying; and that, to Price, was all that mattered.

"Are you - are you all right, pet?" he stammered. It was a stupid question, but it was all he could think of.

There was no reply - except a faint, strangled sobbing.

Price went down on his knees, and stretched out a hand - only to draw it back in horror. It had encountered something flesh-like - perhaps a face, perhaps a hand, but something cold and clammy and obviously very dead.

"My - my God," he said. "What - "

Then the truth dawned on him, and he stood up abruptly.

"Your f-father," he said. "He's . . . "

"Dead, yes," said Anne softly.

Suddenly words were flooding out of her, between hysterical sobs.

Ever since that moment at lunch time, when Price had shown him the ball, Swanleigh had been strange and mono-syllabic. (Perhaps he thought Price had begun to suspect him.) Anne had decided to open the shop after all - chiefly for something to do, and to escape from her father.

She had been standing behind the counter, just before closing time, when suddenly she had seen a ball bouncing around the shop. She was terrified, but not too terrified to realise that it had come from behind her.

She went on, her voice increasingly shaky:

"I looked round - and there *he* was, standing in the doorway behind the counter, a great claw-hammer in his hand. I suddenly realised everything in a flash - he wasn't really paralysed, he was a monster, he'd killed my mother, he'd already tried to kill *me* once before. I lost my head. There was a pair of scissors on the counter. I picked them up . . . there was a struggle . . . I don't know what happened, but . . . but I *could* have driven those scissors right into his chest . . . All I'm sure of is that he gave a low moan - so soft it was almost a sigh - and then there he was, lying on the floor, face-down, at my feet." She was talking now in short, breathless bursts. "I called out to him. There was no reply. I touched his hand. It was cold. I felt his pulse. There didn't seem to be any. I listened for breathing, but there wasn't a sound. I just

179

knelt there beside him, trying to make myself turn him over, but – but terrified at which I'd see. By the time I'd managed to do it, it was pitch dark.''

Ever since then, it seemed, she'd stayed exactly where she was, kneeling by her father's body, held to the spot by a paralysing mixture of guilt, grief, terror and shame. She hadn't moved when she'd heard the phone, or even when Price had come in, although she'd recognised his footsteps and his breathing from the moment he'd walked through the door.

''Over and over again, I kept telling myself that I must get up and turn on the lights, but – but it's no good. I just can't face what I'll see.''

Her voice became totally hysterical.

''No, darling . . . don't *you* turn them on . . . please . . . no . . . NO . . . ''

Price was no longer sweating or shaking. He knew now exactly what he had to do. His voice totally lost its stammer and became clear and commanding.

''Listen, pet. I *am* going to turn on those lights, and you are going to have to look at your father. But I promise you – there's no need to be afraid of what you'll see.'' His tone softened. ''I'll make you another promise. If I have anything to do with it, your days of being afraid are over. For ever.''

Very quietly, before she could even begin to scream ''NO'' again, he turned on the switches. There was an agonising pause of about half a second. Then two powerful fluorescent strips came on above their heads, creating what, after all the darkness, amounted to a blinding blaze of light.

It took Anne's eyes another second to grow accustomed to the glare. It took her rather longer to credit what she was seeing.

There was no sign of any wound on Swanleigh's chest, and not a spot of blood on the pair of scissors that lay beside him. There *was* a rip in his coat near his left armpit; it looked as if the scissors had stabbed there, missing his body altogether.

"I told you there was no need to fear and I meant it," Price said gently. "A man stabbed in the chest doesn't fall on his face. At a guess, I'd say his heart seized up on him during the struggle. *That* would have pitched him forward . . . and in that case, his illness was his killer. Just keep on saying that to yourself – and never, never, never think it was you."

Anne was staring down at her father, her face now showing more grief than terror. It was odd, but in death Swanleigh no longer resembled a Victorian tragedian at all. His eyes were open, but with no suggestion of a wild stare. They looked abstracted, almost as though he was working on some insoluble problem. The years seemed to have rolled away, taking all sickness and melodrama with them, and bringing back Swanleigh the gentle mathematics teacher whom everyone had called Reggie.

Potter suddenly remembered the men waiting outside, and hastily stood up. Too hastily. He accidentally brushed against the plastic toy rack, and to his horror, a dozen rubber balls cascaded down, one of them bouncing right up to Anne, who was still kneeling by her father's body.

She didn't scream, cry or even jump. She simply started to pick them up, and then coolly returned them to the rack.

It was almost, thought Price, as though his promise to her was already being fulfilled.

And that her days of fear *were* over.

19   The Inhuman Factor

When Gideon and Hobbs arrived at the Yard, they found Paul Barnaby waiting for them in the foyer and talking to Matt Honiwell, who had arrived just a minute before them.

The two men were standing by the foyer's most distinctive feature: a stone plinth encased in glass, on top of which a jet of blue flame burnt day and night in memory of the men of the Met who had given their lives in the service of the public.

It felt like twelve years, thought Gideon, not twelve hours since he had last seen Barnaby.

His Acting Deputy Commander had certainly had a gruelling first day in office. In the absence of Gideon himself, and also of the Assistant Commissioner who was his idol, guide and mentor, Barnaby had had to take charge of the whole running of the C.I.D. – and that on a day when one of the most sensational kidnappings in police history had occurred, and the incidents in Whitgate had spread such terror that no one in London had felt entirely safe walking down any street.

It was Barnaby who had had to issue calming statements, and appear on television assuring the public that everything was under control. It was Barnaby who had had to make equally reassuring noises in Scott-Marle's direction - and back them up with detailed plans for containing the Whitgate crisis. It was Barnaby who had had to liaise with the excited Lemaitre, and get him the extra cohorts of C.I.D. men he'd needed. It was Barnaby who had had to get Matt Honiwell the men *he'd* needed, too. The transfer of Derek Price to the Whitgate case, the moving of Potter to Fulham and countless other critical decisions in the course of the day had all been taken by this curious young man who looked as if he would be more at home programming a computer than directing a major fight against crime.

Gideon had to admit that he hadn't done too badly. He particularly appreciated the fact that Barnaby hadn't been bothering him and Hobbs with questions on this anxious day. Realising that they had troubles of their own, he had kept a discreet distance and had simply got on with the job he had been given in his own calm, efficient style.

If only the man wasn't such a cold fish, if only he would just occasionally look, if not like a copper, at least like a human being, Gideon felt that he might actually be proud of his new Acting Deputy.

Despite the fact that it was the end of the hottest May day on record, his shirt looked as crisp as if it were the first thing in the morning; his hair was still as meticulously parted, too. His eyes looked perhaps a shade more watery, due to the mountains of paperwork involved in such a hectic day - but that was all.

"I thought you'd find it more convenient to question Farrant here at the Yard, instead of at Bow Street," he said, addressing Gideon, Hobbs and Honiwell together. "I have arranged for a special room to be prepared – "

"A special room?" Gideon barked.

"Yes, sir. With the video equipment now required for all interrogations under the memo issued by Mr. Hobbs this morning."

Gideon groaned, and looked at his watch.

It was nearly 11.45. He had only minutes to spare before he had to make his Whitgate dash.

"For God's sake, Barnaby, forget all that and let us just see the man, will you?"

Barnaby folded his arms. He looked like a head prefect under orders to subdue an unruly sixth form.

"There is the difficult question of personal involvement. Farrant's lawyers would have a strong victimisation case if he were questioned by the father and grandfather of the kidnapped child. Surely Honiwell here should conduct the video-taped interrogation, and to begin with, I feel, he should see Farrant alone."

Matt reddened. "All Honiwell here wants to do, I can assure you, is get that baby back as soon as possible by fair means or foul."

Hobbs suddenly joined in the conversation – with a passable imitation of a full-scale Gideon roar.

"And where Farrant's concerned, foul means are probably the best. Whether you like it or not, Barnaby, we are all going to see Farrant . . . and the video camera will be switched *off* during the interrogation."

Barnaby's owlish eyes widened to their limits. A statement like that, from Hobbs of all people, was enough to shake his entire world.

"You're joking, of course, sir."

"Do I look as if I'm joking?" Hobbs was really furious now. "The memory of Farrant's own bullying interrogations was one of the reasons why I set up the video experiment in the first place. And I'm not, repeat *not*, going to let it, or anything else, stand in the way of my finding out what the hell he's done with my son. Which room is Farrant in?"

Barnaby hesitated, licking his lips.

Gideon could not help grudgingly admiring him. This curiously inhuman man was standing up to Hobbs, risking his position, perhaps his whole career, for what he believed were human rights. Or was he really only making a lone, last-ditch stand for the new system, the New Broom sweeping clean?

In either event, it was obvious he couldn't win. Alec was advancing on him, looking fully prepared to shake the fact he needed out of him.

"Didn't you hear me, Barnaby? I said, what room – "

Barnaby's resistance crumpled. Looking hurt and resentful at his idol turning out to have feet of clay, he blurted out, "Room one oh three, third floor. If you don't mind, sir, I'd rather not come with you." It was it he couldn't bear to see his beloved video equipment unused.

"We'll survive without you," said Alec, his tone equalling Barnaby's in coldness.

With Matt and Gideon behind him, he turned and strode towards the lifts.

Gideon took one quick glance at Barnaby before they left the foyer.

His new Acting Deputy was still standing in front of the plinth with the blue flame, staring at it unseeingly. Confusion and disillusionment had very rapidly taken their toll. His hair was as dishevelled as if he had actually been running a hand through it, Honiwell style. His expression, even from that distance, looked tired, dazed and strained.

Suddenly he didn't seem to Gideon like a being from another planet any more.

Just a copper – and a pretty good copper at that – fagged out and near nervous exhaustion at the end of a bloody day . . .

"Poor Barnaby," grinned Matt as the lift carried them swiftly to the third floor. "I think he really believes that the Commander of the C.I.D. and the Assistant Commissioner (Crime) are on their way to beat up a suspect."

Alec did not return the smile.

"Unless Farrant comes as clean as the cleanest whistle," he stormed, "Barnaby could be absolutely right."

Even Gideon felt a twinge of alarm at Hobbs's expression as they stepped out of the lift, and went along the corridor in search of Room 103.

*　　　*　　　*

The room was easy to spot; two uniformed constables were on guard outside the door. Inside, they found just a cubbyhole of an office, not dissimilar to the one Farrant himself had had when he had been a Chief Detective Superintendent a year before.

The desk, a plain wooden one, had been pushed against a wall. In the centre of the carpet stood Barnaby's pride and joy – the videotape equipment, complete with a fierce spotlight, which had already been switched on.

Farrant was sitting on the top of the desk, directly in the beam of the spotlight, blearily trying not to blink up at it. His coat was crumpled, and he had no tie. That would have been confiscated when he had been taken in at Bow Street. It wasn't hard to tell where he had been slashed by the carving knife: a wide strip of Elastoplast ran down the left side of his face, from temple to jowl.

The whole scene had a "third-degree" atmosphere, but there was one human touch in it. Somebody had fetched Farrant a carton of coffee, and it was on the desktop beside him, half empty. It was thick black coffee, Gideon noticed, highly suitable for a man who had been brought in drunk.

Farrant stood up when they came in, and immediately started to address them almost as if it were a public meeting. Despite his condition, he had not lost the con man's fluency which had once enabled him to rise so high at Scotland Yard. Neither had he lost that strange, nervous eagerness to please, which showed itself even though he was now face to face with the father and grandfather of the child he had snatched.

"I don't blame you for thinking pretty badly of me, gentlemen, but if you search the H-J filing cabinet in my office, you will find positive proof that I never intended to harm the baby in any way . . . not in any way whatsoever. Nor was I intending to extract a pennyworth of ransom. I was simply – as you might say – *borrowing* the child to act a part in a little drama, a drama which would have hurt nobody, but would have been very important to me in restoring my professional standing."

The sheer cheek of this left even Alec momentarily speechless.

Farrant evidently took this as a sign that he was beginning to impress. His sharp features twisting into a nervous smile, he rushed on, "If everything had gone according to plan, the baby would have been returned two hours ago, sharp on ten o'clock. I couldn't fix the time any earlier, because the 'rescue operation' I had planned to stage required the cover of darkness. For absolute safety, I should have fixed it later, but I was anxious to spare Mrs. Hobbs every minute of worry that I could.''

Hobbs found his voice abruptly. ''You dare to stand there and tell me that you were anxious to spare my wife worry? Good God almighty, man, have you the slightest idea of what you've put her through today?''

Farrant gave the first sign of how heavily he'd been drinking. The ferocity in Alec's voice literally rocked him back on his feet, and he had trouble regaining his balance; for seconds, he was teetering to and fro.

The drink was having another, stranger effect. It seemed to be completely cushioning him from any genuine realisation of the enormity of what he'd done. He might have been discussing a promising business transaction that had unfortunately gone wrong.

''Women can take these things hard, I know. As I've just explained, that's why my plan was carefully conceived to minimise distress - ''

Alec was suddenly dangerously close to losing his self-control.

''You call it minimising distress to steal a ten-day-old baby from a mother who's only been back from hospital for a bare twenty-four hours? And what about Kate Gideon, who was babysitting at the time? She happens to have a weak heart, and she fainted. If it had been more than a faint, Farrant, you'd have been responsible for - for - ''

Alec broke off - probably, thought Gideon, to spare *him* distress.

Farrant was not silenced for a second. He seemed to have a limitless ability to spring to his own defence.

''I could hardly be expected to know such medical particulars,'' he said. ''But I would like to stress again that my

188

intention was only to borrow the baby for ten short hours. No one, I believed, would have to suffer more than . . . let's call it a harassing interlude.''

''My God!'' Alec's voice was suddenly so thick with anger that it sounded as if he had been drinking, too. ''I'll give *you* a harassing interlude – ''

He was obviously on the point of taking a swing at Farrant's face. Matt moved forward, and looked as though he was about to put a restraining hand on Alec's arm. He stopped, perhaps remembering that he was Chief Detective Superintendent and Alec was Assistant Commissioner, or perhaps deciding that Farrant so richly deserved a punch that it would be a pity to intervene.

Gideon, too, thought it would be a pity to intervene, but nevertheless, knew that he had to. A verbal intervention, though, would be better than a physical one. Alec, now his blood was up, couldn't be held back without a scuffle, the sound of which would carry to the two constables outside the door. Probably they would pretend not to hear anything; but Gideon did not want to be part of any situation, ever, in which policemen feigned deafness or ''looked the other way''.

It was an occasion, if ever there was one, for the Gideon roar. But he decided to direct it, not at Hobbs, but at Farrant.

In a voice that almost shook the floor, he shouted, ''Farrant, stop wasting our time with this nonsense. The baby . . . he's with your wife Jill, isn't he? What it's vital for us to know is – *where are they now*?''

At the mention of the baby, Alec forgot his anger, and all his anxiety returned. He drew back, his hand dropping to his side.

At the word ''Jill'', Farrant changed almost as dramatically. The self-justifying confidence man vanished. A brutal criminal took his place - but a broken, self-pitying one. The Farrant flow of words went on.

"Don't talk to me about that bitch, Gideon. She's ruined everything - and I mean every bloody thing! I should have realised that that's what would happen. Every plan stands or falls by - what do the Intelligence people call it - 'the human factor'. In this case, the factor was that someone had to look after the baby for a few short hours - and I was stupid enough to think that I could entrust that task to my dear, sweet wife without her becoming a screaming nutcase. But that's what she turned into at the very first sight of that baby! God knows why . . . but she's always wanted a child, and was probably unbalanced by the fact that she's become pregnant herself. Won't be for long, though. Babies aren't my scene, Gideon. I'm making her see a doctor I know next week, and after that - "

"You're going to force her to have an abortion, are you?" Gideon said. He was beginning to feel that if someone didn't hold him back, he would soon be hitting Farrant himself. His voice became soft - dangerously soft, because it was restrained only by iron self-control. "You call that a human factor? I'd call it an inhuman one. No wonder the poor woman's distraught."

"Distraught? That's not the word I'd use, Gideon . . . not for a silly cow who smashes half the furniture in the house, has a go at me with a carving knife - and keeps screaming that she'll kill herself *and* the baby . . . "

Matt gasped.

Alec's face turned, in the space of a micro-second, from angry red to ghostly white.

Gideon walked slowly past them both, and kept on until he

was actually standing over Farrant, as grave and stern as any judge.

"Be very careful what you say from now on, Farrant. You could be adding a year to your sentence with every lie you tell. This threat that Jill was making. Was she still screaming it when she drove off with the baby?"

"She certainly was," Farrant said. "I was trying to catch her of course, but she slammed the front door in my face, and there was broken glass everywhere . . . I was up to my f . . . . . g ankles in the stuff. By the time I'd got free, she was gone. It was a while before I could work out where she was heading, but as soon as I did, I started off after her."

"Three hours and half a bottle of whisky later, from the look of you," said Gideon contemptuously.

Farrant tried to justify himself as always.

"Well, it took time to change all my plans, and get the Capri back from – "

" – the men who were ready to stage the rescue operation on Barnes Common?" Gideon said.

Farrant stared.

"Then you *did* read that file! My God, there are no flies on you, are there?"

"Never mind all that!" said Alec, with a sudden shout so high-pitched that it was almost a shriek. "Just tell us where you think Jili Farrant has gone with my – my son."

"I'll do more than that, I'll take you there," said Farrant eagerly. Possibly, thought Gideon, he imagined he could help his cause by playing some part in rescuing the baby after all. "It's a flat belonging to her sister Janet. Janet always keeps a room for her there, and she generally goes there when we have our marital ups and downs."

Matt, Alec and Gideon said nothing. They all knew that

was a euphemism for the occasions when Jill had fled from her husband's bullying and battering. They were all trying to decide if Farrant's presence would help or hinder the rescue; and they all came to the same conclusion, voiced by a steely-faced Matt, who had suddenly lost all traces of his "cuddly" look.

"Thank you, Farrant, but we think we'll do better on our own. The only thing we want from you is the address. And you'd better give it to us as quick as a flash. Thirty years you could get, remember, if anything's happened to that child."

It was Farrant's turn to go pale, and he answered very promptly indeed.

"Four seven oh A Strathclyde Tower. That's a high rise block in Hockston," he murmured, and for once it seemed, he had nothing else to say.

But barely a second passed before he recovered.

"Good luck, gentlemen," he called after Gideon, Alec and Matt as they went rushing out of the room.

20   Arrest

Gideon was strongly tempted to accompany Alec and Matt to Hockston, but that would have meant letting Lem down . . . and, if Lem had not been exaggerating, a very great deal more than that. He found it difficult to believe that a speech from him would really prevent a mass shoot out, but if there was any chance that it could, there was no question where he ought to be at midnight.

On Alec's orders, a police car was hastily commandeered, and was already waiting for them as they emerged from the main entrance of Scotland Yard. The fastest route to Hockston happened to be through Whitgate High Street, so Hobbs and Honiwell could drop Gideon on their way.

Gideon looked at his watch as the car swept past the Houses of Parliament and turned into Whitehall.

"Eleven fifty-five," he murmured. "I should be just in time."

"In time for what?" asked Matt, who had not been

keeping up with the extended news bulletins on Whitgate that had been appearing on television all through the day, and was extremely vague about the details of the case.

Gideon was too tense and weary to waste words.

"In time, Matt," he said bluntly, "to stop a lot of shooting – or be shot."

*   *   *

The police car was charging down Whitgate High Street on virtually the stroke of midnight. By then, its siren was wailing and the warning blue light on its roof revolving. The crowd milling all over the street outside the police station reluctantly gave way – and "reluctantly" was the word. They seemed surrounded by angry faces, looking not merely inhuman, but unearthly when caught by flashes from the revolving light. The window on Gideon's left nearly cracked as some metal object – it looked like a beer can – was chucked at the car. Brown blobs of beer spattered the glass; they were joined by beads of saliva as two skinheads leant forward and spat at the car from about two inches away.

"They are a lot of charmers around here, aren't they?" said Matt.

A uniformed constable beside the driver was incensed by all this disrespect for the Law.

"Shall I get out and nab a few of these bastards for you, sir?"

"No," said Gideon sharply. "Not unless you want them to stop spitting – and start firing."

The constable whistled.

"You don't mean they've all got guns, sir?"

"That's just what I do mean, I'm afraid," Gideon said. To the driver, he added, "Pull in as close to the police station as you can. I'd like my walk inside to be as short as possible. I've never minded spit and polish – but can do without spit and Double Diamond all over my suit . . . "

In fact, it was spared this embellishment.

The moment Gideon climbed out, a gasp went round the crowd, who recognised him instantly, even though they could only glimpse his massive frame in silhouette against the revolving blue light on the car.

"Christ, they've sent us bloody Gideon himself," said the skinhead who had spat at the window.

"Give 'im everything you've got!" someone else commanded.

But it took nerve to spit or throw things at a living legend, and before anyone in the crowd could summon up the necessary courage, Gideon was across the pavement and inside the police station, where he found a very anxious Lemaitre awaiting him.

"Blimey, Gee Gee, you've cut it fine. I've a feeling the balloon's going to go up here at any second. Come with me and I'll show you what I mean."

Lemaitre took Gideon up to his first-floor office. The window, with one pane shattered by a bullet, was a stark reminder of the dangerous situation below. Lem turned the lights off, and together, he and Gideon looked out on a crowd of about a hundred yelling and fist-waving youths. The crowd was self-segregated into two groups of roughly equal size, separated by about three yards of pavement. Both groups carried bloodthirsty emblems, which they held up proudly in the orange light of the street lamps. The leader of one group – presumably the Strode supporters – was brandishing a scaffold-like structure on which hung an effigy with a placard reading: "STRING UP CAXTON - THE RED

ASSASSIN!'' The other group – obviously Caxtonites – had a bloodstained pillow held aloft on the end of a rifle and bayonet. The pillow had a crude drawing of a military-looking face on it, and the attached placard read, ''DEATH TO STRODE – THE FASCIST PIG!'' Both groups were alternating between shaking their fists in the direction of the police station and hurling abuse at each other.

Gideon had seen many riots in his time, some of them involving thousands of angry men and women. But he had never seen one that alarmed him as much as this. The effigies of the hanging Caxton and the beheaded Strode; the roars of hatred, as continuous and as steadily rising as an incoming tide; the sea of young faces, their expressions only dimly discernible from this height, but seeming to register nothing but a mindless fury – all this, added to the knowledge that in the pockets of this murderous mob were something approaching a hundred guns, made Gideon's mouth run dry.

''We've not a lot of time to waste, have we?'' murmured Lemaitre. ''The sooner this lot are told the truth – that they're making all this song and dance about nothing, because Fordyce was killed by a pot-shot loony – ''

''*If he was*,'' said Gideon, so urgently that even Lemaitre couldn't ignore the objection. ''It's an important point, Lem. Because I don't rate myself very highly as a con man, and I've got to be *convinced* of something before I can put it over.''

Lem stared.

''Come off it, Gee Gee. You know as well as I do that all the trouble here was started by some villain distributing guns to yobos in the Screen Scene cinema. I know I pulled in Caxton and Strode for questioning, but that was more to stop a lynching than to interrogate them about the shooting. Though I have been quizzing both of them about whether they had any supporters who were fanatical, and hell-bent on starting a civil war."

Gideon groaned. Once Lem got an idea into his head, it took a very great deal of shifting. He had been propounding this maniac-aiming-to-start-a-war theory for almost the whole day, and still seemed stone deaf to anything that challenged it. But it had to be challenged – and now.

"Tell me, Lem," he said. "Why are you so *sure* that the assassin was just a pot-shooter?"

For the first time, Lem seemed defensive.

"Well," he said, "I watched him in action myself. He was on that Underground roof over there, behind the London Transport sign. And he blazed off crazily in all directions . . . completely at random, as far as I could see. It was just bad luck on Sir Gilbert Fordyce that his forehead happened to get in the way of one of the bullets."

Gideon stared thoughtfully at the spot Lem had indicated.

"That's a very clever place for a subnormal yobbo to choose," he said softly. "It looks to me much more like the sort of vantage point a highly skilled assassin would pick." Very deliberately, he went on, "An assassin who wanted to be mistaken for a pot-shooter . . . and who had covered himself beforehand by deliberately causing pot-shot incidents all over the area."

Lemaitre gasped.

"You – you mean – "

"I mean," said Gideon, even more deliberately, "that I think it's very possible that the assassin and the gun distributor are one and the same person. Presumably, a fanatical Jeremy Caxton supporter."

"You wouldn't find Caxton agreeing with you about that," Lem said. "He claims – very vehemently indeed – that

197

Fordyce was shot on the orders of his own deputy, Major
Strode. There was no love lost between Strode and Fordyce,
Caxton swears. And, of course, with Fordyce gone, Strode
has taken over as undisputed leader of the Right."

"We seem to be getting deeper and deeper into politics at
their nastiest," Gideon grunted. "I suppose this Major Strode
claims equally vehemently that Caxton was behind the
shooting."

"Strangely enough, he doesn't, Gee Gee. He's a
surprisingly unmilitant type, the Major, in some ways. I got
the impression that privately he takes my view that it was a
pot-shot killing. It's hard for him to say, though – because he
wasn't on the scene himself at the time."

Gideon tensed.

"He wasn't? Then where the hell was he?"

"Down that alley beside the Underground station –
parking his car, so he says." Lem was suddenly equally tense.
"Though now I come to think of it, it's a very odd place to
park one. It's a cul-de-sac, with hardly any turning space –
and unless you're prepared to back all the way out . . . ''

He broke off, and both he and Gideon found themselves
staring hard at the spot on the roof where the assassin had
been, and thinking the same thing: what an easy jump it was
up from – or down to – that alley.

"Tell me exactly what happened after the assassination,"
Gideon breathed.

"There was a moment of total hysteria, and I mean total,"
said Lem. "People were firing shots in all directions – that's
when this window got hit. I was out on the street by then –
just in time to see some lynch-happy Fordyce men making a
dead set at Caxton, who was at the top of the steps. Suddenly
Strode came charging out of the alley, telling the lynch mob

that they were all bloody fools, and ought to realise that the assassin had been just a pot-shooter.''

"Exactly what he would have said," murmured Gideon, "if he was the assassin himself, and had been deliberately firing pot-shots to give that very impression. What happened then?''

"A boy called Johnson – the poor kid was in a shocking state, I think he'd been a pet henchman of Fordyce's – staged a big dramatic scene. Pointed to Fordyce's forehead, and claimed that only a skilled assassin could have been as accurate as that. Strode did a hurried about face, and shouted that he realised he'd been wrong. He pulled out a gun and seemed all set to lead the lynching – but I stepped in, and started to lead *him* – towards the police station.''

"Did you get the gun?" asked Gideon. "It ought to go straight to Ballistics if you did.''

Lem's voice became more and more hesitant.

"No. Strode's boys started to play funny games . . . they passed the gun round and round in a circle . . . I didn't bother that much, because Strode had shown me it was unloaded.''

"As it would have been if he'd just emptied it from that roof!" Gideon was glowering. "You let a vital piece of evidence slip through your fingers there, Lem. That gun could have cracked the whole case. But now it's out there amongst a hundred guns . . . as impossible to find as a pebble on a beach . . . ''

Gideon turned from the window, and started to pace up and down the unlighted office. He was struggling to think, but the growing din from the mobs outside made it difficult. It was like trying to concentrate while tossing about on a stormy sea; a sea that could at any moment unleash a floodtide of violent death.

Was he falling into the Lemaitre trap and jumping to conclusions about this Major Strode? The case against the man was beginning to seem formidable, but it was still purely circumstantial. It could have been a coincidence that he had happened to emerge from that alley. He might have had quite an innocent motive for being so quick to get rid of that gun. If only there was a shred of real evidence . . .

The door opened, a dazzling shaft of light from the corridor slashing across the room, and a young man entered. A very young man, it seemed to Gideon: in the near darkness, he could almost have been mistaken for one of the yobbos. He seemed in a state of great excitement, and almost ran across to Lemaitre.

"Excuse me, sir, but there's something I think you ought to know straight – "

He broke off, his jaw dropping almost comically as he noticed Gideon. He recognised him instantly, even through the gloom.

"Don't be afraid, Blake," Lem chuckled. "Commander Gideon won't bite you. Unless you deserve it – in which case, he'll ruddy well have you for breakfast!"

"Blake!" said Gideon. "Aren't you the Detective Sergeant who encountered the gun distributor in the cinema – and nearly got handed a gun yourself?"

"That's right, sir." Blake was obviously pleased and flattered to be remembered.

"Tell me," Gideon shouted. Shouting was now the only way to be heard above the noises from the street outside. "How good a look did you take at that man? Do you think you could recognise him if you saw him again?"

Blake's answer, also shouted, coincided with a lull in the shouting and jeering of the crowd, which was perhaps why it reached Gideon's ears with stunning force.

"I not only *can* – I *have* recognised him, sir. That's what I came to tell Superintendent Lemaitre. Just a moment ago, I happened to be passing Interrogation Room Three down-stairs, when the door was opened and I caught a glimpse of the man inside. I haven't a shadow of doubt that it's him!"

"Interrogation Room Three?" said Lem. Suddenly he was too excited to stand on ceremony. "Blimey, Gee Gee, this proves you're right – all the way along the line That's where I've been questioning Strode. And I left him there as a matter of courtesy. Didn't want to clap a political V.I.P. in the cells."

Gideon walked over to the door and switched on the lights. In this part of the room, they were relatively safe from beer cans, bullets or flying glass; and in any case, he was in no mood to bother about safety.

"Lem," he shouted. "Bring Strode up here. I want to go out and tell that mob that the assassin's been arrested . . . and before I do, I'd like to make that statement true."

*   *   *

Lemaitre went out without another word and less than a minute later he was back with Strode. Despite his hours of interrogation, the Major was still looking remarkably spruce in a faultlessly-pressed grey suit. He was, in fact a study in grey, with a trim grey moustache, greying hair cut short back and sides, and very cold grey eyes that gave no hint of what he was thinking at all.

He stood stiffly to attention, with Lemaitre on one side and Blake on the other, while Gideon formally arrested him on three charges; unlawfully distributing weapons and inciting youths to commit murder, as well as assassinating Fordyce.

201

Gideon was not sure that, at this stage, he could make all the charges stick. The important thing was that a formal arrest should be made, and announced to the crowd. It would of course, be inviting uproar to mention the arrested man's name. But if he could say, with all the authority at his command, "Go home. The culprit's been found, and is behind bars . . . "

The roar of the crowd was suddenly louder, more menacing even than before. To it was added the crash of breaking glass as a bottle, or some other object, smashed through one of the ground-floor windows. Unless he acted very fast indeed, the first shot would be fired any second now. And he would have no choice but to order Lemaitre to send out the force of armed policemen waiting in the station below . . . No choice, in other words, but to launch a full-scale shooting war.

"Take him to the cells," Gideon barked over his shoulder to Lemaitre and Blake as he headed for the door. "I have a rather urgent job to do outside."

"Outside, Commander?" said Strode unexpectedly. "Do I understand that you're going to try to placate my followers – and those Caxton animals, too? I'd very much like to know how."

Gideon turned in the doorway and stared straight into those expressionless grey eyes.

"By telling them that the assassin has been arrested and Fordyce avenged," he said.

Strode raised a very correct military eyebrow.

"You haven't a hope in hell of being believed, you know," he shouted, adding, after a significant pause, "Unless *I* come out there with you and support all you say."

Gideon started. There was no denying that that was probably true.

"You'd be willing to do that?"

"Certainly, Commander. My best chance of persuading you to drop these ridiculous charges is surely to convince you that I am a man of peace . . . "

Pull the other one, Gideon thought grimly. It's got bells on it. Suddenly, he needed no telling what game Strode was really playing. Out there on the station steps, he would be at close quarters with his followers, backed, one could almost say, by fifty loaded guns. If, under cover of being about to make a speech, he stepped forward – and then turned that forward step into a sudden dash into the crowd . . .

There was one way, though, to scotch that little scheme. It wouldn't be so easy for him to make that sudden dash from a first-floor window . . .

Gideon slowly walked back into the room, and kept on walking until he was at the window, staring down at the crowd. Now that the lights were on, they could see his silhouette, and were suddenly staring back at him.

A silence fell – one of the most ominous silences that Gideon had ever known.

He opened the window wide, slivers of glass from its broken pane cascading down on to the pavement. The tinkle was as startlingly audible as the proverbial pin dropping.

So was Gideon's voice as he said, quietly and conversationally, "Can you all hear me down there? Good. I've an announcement to make that I think you'll find interesting."

He did not want to make it too easy for them to hear. He wanted them to have to strain to listen. And the trick worked, at any rate for the moment. There was hardly a whisper, or even a rustle, anywhere in the crowd. Only two things moved on the whole scene: the effigy of the hanging Jeremy Caxton, which continued to swing to and fro, its head lolling sideways with a nauseating realism, and the camera of a distant TV newsman, who was focusing a zoom lens on the scene from the steps of the Civic Centre on the other side of the street. Gideon was relieved to see the camera. The thought that there would be ten or twenty million witnesses to any act of violence they committed might restrain the more intelligent youths down there; although, if he failed to keep the temperature down, that factor couldn't be counted on. Even the watching eye of a TV camera couldn't be seen through a red mist of hate . . .

And the hate was beginning to surface again.

"Nothing the f . . . . . g fuzz had got to say is interesting to us!" shrieked one youth, in front of the crowd. A lot of faces turned toward him, suggesting he was a kind of leader – probably, Gideon thought, Fordyce's dramatic ex-henchman, Johnson. "We don't want your lies and soft soap, Gideon. We want the truth – from the only man we can trust to speak it. We want Strode!"

Before the rest of the BGBM followers could take up the chant – which would probably be immediately met with chants of "We want Jeremy" from the Caxtonites, and perhaps start bullets flying – Gideon replied, still quietly and casually:

"Don't worry. In just a minute, you're going to get him."

That startled the crowd into another silence. Gideon decided to make full use of it. It could well be the last.

Raising his voice now, to give the announcement all the official weight he could, he told them, "The man who shot Sir Gilbert Fordyce is under arrest, and will appear at the North London Magistrate's Court at ten thirty tomorrow morning. His name will be released in due course – "

"In due course?" said a mocking voice beside him. "Why

be so reticent, Commander? *I'm* quite willing to release it now!''

Lemaitre had brought Strode up to the window, no doubt after his, Gideon's, promise to the BGBM mob that they were going to get their leader in a minute.

Now Strode was actually leaning out and waving down at his supporters, who raised a massive cheer at the sight of him - countered, of course, by jeers from the Caxtonites. There was suddenly a menacing development. The BGBM men pressed forward, until they were solidly massed under the window, having pushed their opponents to the rear.

Strode had only to jump, thought Gideon - a lesser jump than the one he had made from the Underground roof - and he would be in the centre of a protecting circle of fifty or more armed youths.

''*I'm* the man they've arrested!'' Strode was saying, and now his voice was no longer mocking, but a full parade-ground bark. ''It's a plot by the Commie pigs behind today's Scotland Yard. Are you going to let them get away with it?''

The roar of fury that came welling up seemed to rock the whole building; it did, in fact, shake a few more slivers of glass out of the window. But far more alarming than the roar was the glinting of metal on all sides, as guns appeared in fifty hands.

''Come on down, Major,'' Johnson yelled. ''We'll look after you.''

Strode was halfway over the sill now, prepared to jump.

Gideon seized him by one arm and the back of his collar, but the Major, probably the most experienced man there in unarmed combat, writhed, kicked out backwards, and was suddenly almost free.

Forgetting that he wasn't *quite* free, that Gideon's hand

was still like an iron clamp round the collar of his jacket, Strode jumped . . . to find himself dangling in midair, his feet about a yard and a half off the pavement below.

It only lasted a second, that dangling – and even that took all of Gideon's massive strength.

But it was long enough for one youth at the front of the crowd. A youth who was rather different from the BGBM supporters around and behind him. He was younger than most of them too, being no more than five foot three. And his chalk-white, mask-like face concealed different and far more dangerous emotions.

He had no interest in politics, Left or Right.

He did not recognise the Major, even though it was he who had given him his gun.

He had only one thought in his deranged, subnormal brain.

The dangling man made a beautifully helpless target.

He took his revolver out of his pocket, levelled it at the Major's heart . . . and following his favourite precept, shot to kill.

21   Avenger

The force of the bullet caused the dangling Strode to give a convulsive leap; the shock made Gideon let go. Strode's body dropped, to fall lifeless at his killer's feet, latest victim of the pot-shot mania that he himself had created.

The killer himself looked coolly up at Gideon's window. In the light shining down from it, the mask-like face could be seen in detail. Only the eyes showed emotion; and they were glittering with an insane sense of triumph.

"Christ Almighty," breathed Lem. "You know who he is, Gee Gee? He's the 'shoot-to-kill' bastard who got Constable Morton this morning. Fits the description Charlie gave me exactly . . . If we don't stop him quick, he could go berserk and . . . "

Gideon's blood turned first cold, then glacial at the thought of what that meant. A "shoot-to-kill" maniac on the rampage amongst two armed mobs, one of them already at fever pitch because they had seen their leader die . . . It was a situation that could develop in seconds into a wholesale bloodbath.

Unless, before those seconds elapsed, he acted – and showed the crowd that instant murder brought instant arrest.

Just as Strode had done a minute before, Gideon heaved a leg over the sill and prepared to jump.

Lem caught hold of his arm.

"For God's sake, Gee Gee, *no*. You can't tackle him yourself. You aren't even armed . . . "

But Gideon, too, proved expert at wriggling free.

He landed right beside Strode's body, breathless and jarred with the shock of the drop. Before he could recover, the killer had thrust the muzzle of his gun against his chest. It was still hot from the last shot it had fired; the smell of cordite mingled with that of scorching cloth from Gideon's coat – both very direct reminders that he was dealing with no ordinary criminal, but a pathological case who had just killed, and was itching to kill again.

Behind and above him, from the direction of the open window, Gideon could hear Lem shouting orders. In a minute – perhaps less – there would be armed men at the window, who would have the drop on this blood-crazy youth. Around him, amongst the BGBM mob, there was a strange, strained silence, partly, he imagined, due to fear, partly to a conflict of emotions. The hated Gideon had landed right in front of them, but he had come to avenge their leader, arrest his killer. Should they spit at him or lend a hand? By common consent, they seemed to be deciding to do neither, but just shuffled back as far as they could, stonily watching. This left Gideon and the killer standing by the wall of the police station, in a half-circle of cleared space – a very small half-circle, with a radius of less than a yard.

He must play for time, Gideon thought . . . somehow – anyhow, play for just that crucial sixty seconds of time . . .

But then he looked into the killer's eyes and saw an expression he had never seen before, even on a murderer's face – intense excitement and anticipation, as though the thought of firing gave the boy almost a sexual thrill.

At the sight of that, Gideon knew that there was nothing he could do or say that would buy him any time at all.

The silence dragged on, becoming almost unbearable before it was broken – by the echoing click of the safety catch going back on the revolver.

Well, at least he would go out fighting, thought Gideon.

He seized the gun with his right hand and struggled to force the muzzle upwards; at the same time, he brought his right knee up into the youth's stomach. All the while, he expected to hear a deafening roar; to feel searing pain, or worse, a great numbness in his chest . . .

The roar came, not merely deafening him, but seeming to split his skull in two. It was accompanied by the smell of cordite, so strong that it choked and half-blinded him.

For a moment his fear reached such a pitch that he seemed to have been exploded out of Time itself, and just stood, paralysed, waiting for the pain – or the numbness – to start.

Neither did.

Instead his clearing vision showed him the young killer lying on the pavement, twitching and writhing, blood pouring from a gaping wound in the small of his back. He had been shot at such close range that, even in the orange light from the street lamps, black scorch marks showed on his T-shirt all round the wound.

In a second, the writhing and the twitching stopped. With a faint final moan, the youth lay still.

"F . . . . . g hell," someone muttered, in a voice hoarse with fear and horror.

Gideon looked up - and saw the youth whom he had identified as Johnson standing, a smoking revolver in his hand, staring down at the corpse he'd just created.

There was no triumph, though, in *his* eyes. He was shaking all over, and tears were actually streaming down his face.

"Thank you," Gideon said quietly. "Another second there, and I'd have been a gonner."

"I didn't do it for you, you f . . . . . g fuzz pig," Johnson choked. "It was because of what he did to Strode."

Gideon suddenly remembered what Lem had told him about this Johnson - that he had been a close follower of Sir Gilbert Fordyce and very shaken by his death. Obviously he had transferred his hero-worship to the Major, and had accepted without question Strode's lies about his arrest being a Communist plot.

It was time to force him to face the ironic truth that he had just avenged Sir Gilbert's assassin. He was in a bad enough state already; such a state that Gideon guessed that this was the first time in his life that he'd fired a gun, perhaps the first time he'd even touched or seen one.

"Killing brought no thrills to you, I can see," Gideon said gently.

"What the bloody hell do you think I am - a pot-shooter like him?" Johnson raged. Then suddenly all the aggression went out of him, as fast as air from a pricked balloon. "Though maybe you're right, and there isn't much to choose between us. One thing's for sure. Our victims are just as dead." His voice broke. He was startlingly close to sobbing. "I'm sick of the whole f . . . . . g shooting bit. Never want to see a gun again as long as I live."

Gideon glanced round at the circle of youths, standing and watching them. He expected to hear a murmur of contempt

210

for such a display of softness; to see raised fists, sneering faces, hate-filled eyes. Instead, wherever he looked, he seemed to see expressions of uneasiness and half-concealed horror. Was it an effect of the street lighting, which was reducing so many of the faces to vague orange blurs, or could the sight of two sickening killings, in quick succession, have changed the whole mood of these mobs?

It was possible. After all, they were leaderless. With Strode and Fordyce dead, and Caxton out of the picture, there was no one to rally their morale, to restore their nerves with a verbal fix of hate and fury.

Gideon's spirits rose – to be abruptly dashed by the sounds of shouted commands from the police station behind him. It was clear what was happening. Lemaitre had decided that order had to be restored whatever the risk, and had asked Inspector Skelton to bring out the hundred-strong contingent of uniformed men. The next moment, streams of them were pouring down the station steps, moving out first to mingle with the mobs, and then to make a human cordon round them.

The constables were not only armed, they were making a great show of their revolvers, almost brandishing them . . . which could hardly be more stupid, Gideon thought. Whatever the general mood of the mobs, there were bound to be some bloody-minded youths who would reply by brandishing their own guns, and then –

Two shots rang out, one from somewhere to Gideon's right, and the other close at hand on his left. A youth started screaming and staggering about; it looked as though, in trying to draw his gun, he had shot himself in the leg. What had happened on the right he couldn't see – and could only pray that it was a similarly abortive incident.

Johnson seemed to be as horrified as Gideon by what he heard.

"The bloody fools," he said. "We've had *enough* shooting here, enough for a lifetime."

"Then come and help me tell them so," Gideon said. Taking Johnson's arm, and almost dragging the youth behind him, he forced his way through the mob to the station steps, which were clear of the stream of uniformed men by now, and climbed to the top of them.

"Listen to me, all of you," he bellowed, his voice carrying effortlessly to every part of the crowded street. Something in his tone commanded attention; even the boy with the injured leg stopped screaming to listen. "If you want to turn this place into an Okay Corral, that is perfectly okay with the police. We're ready for you. We have as many guns as you have. And we're trained to use them, which most of you aren't. There's another advantage which we have, which you may call an unfair one, but it's a fact of life. If a constable fires at one of you, he's doing his duty and could even get a medal for it. If you fire at a constable you're committing attempted murder against an officer of the law, and there isn't a magistrate in London who wouldn't give you five to ten years for an offence like that. Just being caught with a gun on you can get you put away for a long, long time. And since you're entirely surrounded, you're *all* going to be caught with guns on you . . . unless you take advantage of a little offer I'm making. Any gun that arrives on these steps at my feet within the next thirty seconds will be counted as a voluntary contribution to the public safety, and will be gratefully received, with no questions asked. And Mr. Johnson here will, I believe, make the first donation."

"Glad to," Johnson muttered, and hurled his gun down

the steps as eagerly as if it was blistering his fingers.

It was at that point that Gideon began to sense that things were going wrong.

Perhaps Johnson had thrown the gun away *too* eagerly; perhaps it looked to them as though he had turned traitor and started collaborating with the enemy. Or perhaps he, Gideon, had taken the wrong tone, and sounded too truculent and threatening.

For whatever reason, there was a sudden, subtle but unmistakable change in the atmosphere. The silence had been attentive. Now it was sullen and menacing.

Five, eight, ten seconds passed, and Johnson's gun remained the only one on the steps.

Gideon looked up - and suddenly saw why.

Lemaitre (or Skelton) had overdone things. They had stationed armed policemen at every window, right along the first floor of the police station. Upwards of twenty revolvers - together with some rifles and shotguns - were trained on the pavement and the station steps.

It was impossible to approach the steps without coming into almost point-blank range of these weapons - in other words, into the absolute power of the police. It not only looked like a trap. Throwing down a gun under such circumstances would not be a dignified gesture - and it would be a pathetic surrender to the hated "pigs", and involve an unthinkable loss of face for BGBM supporters and Caxtonites alike.

There was only one answer, thought Gideon: the police had to make a gesture too. Which led him to perhaps the most daring decision of his career.

"I see you all have doubts about unilateral disarmament," he shouted. "All right then - we'll make it multilateral.

Every revolver that you throw will be matched by one from the police side . . . starting with the guns in those windows . . . ''

That did it.

The sullen silence was broken, first by the clatter of gun after gun cascading on the steps and then, as dazed-looking constables came forward and added their weapons to the growing pile, by a sound that left Gideon completely baffled.

He thought it was a roar of anger at first, or perhaps a massive continuous jeer. It took Johnson to reveal the staggering truth.

"Do you hear that? They're f . . . . . g well cheering!'' he said.

The sudden awe on his face as he looked at Gideon suggested that he had found his third hero to worship that day.

*   *   *

Gideon was rarely able to enjoy a triumph for long, and this occasion was no exception.

He felt a tug at his sleeve, and looked round to see a troubled-looking Lemaitre behind him.

"Sorry to interrupt, Gee Gee,'' he said. "If ever there was a man of the moment, it's you – but I've got Matt Honiwell on the phone, calling from Hockston. He swears it's very urgent. In fact, the word he used was 'desperate'.''

22   Gideon's Way

Gideon rushed into the police station, the warm glow inside him changing to its very opposite: a freezing sense of dread.

There was no Chief Detective Superintendent with more experience at handling crises than Matt Honiwell – and he had Alec with him, as well. If a situation had arisen with which both of them together couldn't cope, then "desperate" was the word for it indeed.

It took a very agitated Matt – strangely hoarse, and speaking so fast that he was almost gabbling – a bare twenty seconds to spell it out.

Soon after they had arrived at the flat – while, in fact, they had still been arguing with her sister Janet in the doorway – Jill Farrant had developed full-scale suicidal hysteria. With the baby in her arms, she had rushed out on to the balcony, where there was only a slender metal balustrade between her, the baby and a drop of twenty storeys, or more than 250 feet.

Before anyone realised what she was doing, she had actually clambered over the balustrade and tried to hurl herself and the baby down. But at the very last moment, panic had paralysed her. She had seized hold of the rail behind her, and clung on. And she was still clinging on - with her one free hand, because her other arm was still clasped round the baby. Who was wriggling and -

That was all Gideon needed to hear, or could, in fact, stand hearing.

Lem had a police car waiting and within seconds it was hurtling him towards Hockston. Afterwards, he was unable to remember any part of that journey. It was as though Life had become a surrealistic film, where one nightmare moment blurred into another - Matt's agitated voice on the phone turning into the real Honiwell standing in the flat doorway, with nothing but a succession of vague images in between.

The real Matt looked not merely agitated, but perilously close to panic.

"She's still holding on, but only just, George. Alec's out there on the balcony, but doesn't dare to go within a yard of her now. The one time he tried to take the baby, she screamed and snatched it back so violently that she nearly let go of it - and the balcony rail too . . . "

There were more vague images. A wildly untidy living room. Janet, Jill Farrant's sister, hunched in a chair with her hands covering her mouth to stifle sobs. Alec, not only looking shaken, but actually shaking as Gideon strode past him on the balcony, with Matt following behind.

It was a cheerless balcony, obviously never used as such. There were no chairs or tables out there - just a cheap, tinny-looking balustrade about three feet high, edging one side of a bare grey concrete floor, which was dimly illuminated by a forty-watt bulb set in an equally bare concrete ceiling. In this feeble light, Gideon had to go almost right up to the rail before he could make out the face of Jill Farrant, staring wildly at him from out of the darkness – and that of the baby George, who seemed to be giving his famous version of the Gideon glare. Both Jill and the baby were no more than a tantalising arm's length away.

From what Matt had said, Gideon had expected them to be literally hanging, with no support except those five white fingers that he could see gripping the rail at the top of the balustrade. But the concrete floor did project an inch or so beyond the balustrade, and this was giving Jill a toehold, even though a terrifyingly precarious one.

Without that, he doubted if she could have lasted a minute out there. As it was, the thought of the strain those fingers had borne – and of how long they had been bearing it – made Gideon instinctively reach out towards them, to give what support he could.

"Stop it!" Jill Farrant screamed, and Gideon very reluctantly let his hand fall to his side. "I know what you're trying to do. You just want to get near enough to snatch the baby, that's all."

Gideon studied what he could see of her face in the darkness. When they had last met, at some C.I.D. social function, she had struck him as a fluffy blonde type, all softness and silliness, but with curiously hard eyes. Now the fluffiness and softness seemed to have gone, leaving the hardness and silliness – both intensified by the hysteria.

But hard women didn't get obsessive over babies, Gideon thought. The hardness had therefore to be a shell, which could be cracked, if he went the right away about it.

"I promise you," he said, "that I have no intention of

snatching that baby. At this height, it would be far too risky a thing to do. In any case, I have a feeling that he's really in very safe hands.''

"Safe hands?'' Her laugh was half a hysterical sob. "Who do you think you're fooling? I've nearly dropped him half a dozen times.''

"But you never did drop him, did you – even though your arm must be half wrenched out of its socket by the effort of holding on to him . . . No, Mrs. Farrant. You won't convince me that any baby is not safe with you.''

The girl seemed completely nonplussed . . . and had been made to realise just how agonising the ache in that arm had become.

"Here,'' she said suddenly. "Take him – for God's sake.'' Very bitterly she added, half to herself, "All he's doing anyway is holding up the action.''

She twisted round so that the baby was pressed against the rail, his nose in fact touching it.

"Go on, grab him,'' she said. "Quick, I can't hold on – much longer . . . ''

It was, for Gideon, the most terrible moment of the night. If that last remark about "holding up the action'' had meant what he thought it did, then the moment he took George, the girl would let go of the rail; and he couldn't buy life, even the most precious life, at the cost of someone's certain death.

Very, very gruffly, he said, "I'll grab him only if you'll let me grab you too.''

The girl's white face registered total disbelief. From somewhere behind him, he heard Alec gasp with almost equal incredulity.

"George!'' he whispered. "George, you can't – ''

218

"Quiet," Gideon snapped back. "Let me handle this."

Alec did not complain any more. It was suddenly obvious that Gideon's approach was right. The realisation that whether she lived or died really mattered to him - mattered so much that he was gambling the life of his own grandson - had brought a sudden startling change in Jill.

Her eyes lost their wildness and filled with tears.

"All right, Commander. You can get us both out of this . . . together . . ."

Gently, Gideon took the baby from her, and handed him over to his father. Then he helped Jill to climb over the balustrade and back, at last, into the safety of the balcony.

He expected her to be a sobbing, hysterical wreck. But the double assurance that she had received - that she mattered, and that she was a born mother - had left her, for the moment at least, strangely calm and poised.

The first thing she did, after reaching safety, was to help herself, without permission, to the handkerchief from Gideon's top pocket. The second thing she did was to walk across to Alec and stare at the baby as it lay in his arms.

"Just wanted to make sure I hadn't hurt him," she said. "And - and I haven't, have I? Look . . . there's not a bruise, not a scratch . . . and he's not even frightened of me. It's - it's as though we'd been playing a game together." Suddenly her calmness had vanished, and her tears were coming in floods. "I'm not excusing what I did. Hell, there's *no* excuse! But please believe me - I didn't really know *what* I was doing . . . It made me so mad - literally mad, I suppose - to think that I can never be a mother."

"Who says that you can never be a mother?" asked Gideon, although he knew the answer all too well.

A touch of hysteria returned to Jill Farrant's eyes. "John

won't hear of it. I'm pregnant *now* – but he's – he's insisting . . . "

"I very much doubt if he'll be in a position to insist on anything for a good few years," Gideon told her. "And after that, it's up to you whether he insists on anything where you're concerned again."

The relief in Jill Farrant's eyes was remarkable to see.

She turned to Alec and started to make faces at the baby – who, astonishingly, started to chuckle.

"I know it's a lot to ask – but would you trust me to hold him once more just for a second . . . to say goodbye?"

Hobbs glared angrily, and was obviously about to say "Not on your life!" Then suddenly he shrugged and smiled.

"If Commander Gideon feels it's all right," he said.

"But you're the father. Why do you ask him?"

Alec's reply was directed as much to Gideon and Matt as it was to Jill.

Drawing himself up to his full height, and with all his old smoothness and polish suddenly returning, he murmured wryly, "Because, Mrs. Farrant, as I shall never stop reminding myself, and everyone else, from now on, it pays to do things – Gideon's way."